A Curate in Love

A Curate in Love

RICHARD HUGHES

ember

Published by Ember Press 2023
www.emberprojects.co.uk

ISBN: 978-1-7392844-4-2

 A CIP catalogue record for this book is available from the British Library

Cover illustration by Millree Hughes
Cover design and typesetting: Megan Sheer
Printed by Severn, Gloucester

I would like to thank many people,
Anne Weisman, Mike Poulton and Jeffrey Olstead in particular, for their help
and encouragement during the writing of
A Curate in Love.

Contents

CHAPTER 1

The die is cast

Imagine the solemnity of it, my concluding interview with the Right Reverend James Charles John Bartholomew, Doctor of Divinity, Lord Bishop of St Asaph, on the eve of my ordination to the deaconate, Trinity Sunday, 1st June 1958. I remember it well. It was like walking into a scene from El Greco, the neo-Gothic gloom of the Gladstone Library, in his purple cassock the plump, turkey-like figure of the bishop, his hair like so many tiny flames, 'There you are, Richard,' he said. 'I want your signature.'

A pen was thrust into my hand, the great ledger set out before him. Nothing further was said, the consequences unexplained. I was signing away my civil rights. Before it hadn't been illegal for me to commit adultery. Now I could be brought before an ecclesiastical court. It's not, I might add, something I'd done . . . and not for fear of the courts. It would have betrayed my love for Ann.

But there were also advantages to a man's membership of holy orders, as was suggested while I was a student at the University College, Bangor. Coming away from St Mary's Teacher Training College on the high ridge above the city was a decrepit Morris Eight driven by the Reverend Horace Bowen-Owen, earnest, black-suited, eminent poet and member of the Gorsedd.[1] With him was the ostentatiously soutaned,[2] outrageously gay Father Tom, Anglican chaplain to the university. The brakes failed. The car gathered momentum, speeding downhill with ever accelerating rapidity to run smack into WH Smith's on the High Street. Miraculously nobody was hurt. A crowd gathered. A policeman tried to disperse them. But Father Tom possessed the power of the ordinal. 'Let us pray,' he said. With that the crowd was gone.

So, the long ponderous ceremony of my ordination came and went and with it my life was changed. Thereafter I was assistant curate of Mold, a sprawling market town some twelve miles southwest of Chester, markedly different from the two years of my immediate past at the theological college of St Michael and all Angels in Llandaff on the outskirts of Cardiff. I was in familiar surroundings, though. Most curates were parachuted in, like the apostles of old, sent as strangers and sojourners into an unknown land, but my father was vicar of the nearby parish of Cilcain, so my teenage years had been spent as a pupil at the Alun School on Alexandra Road.

'Nothing further is expected of you this evening, Mr Hughes,' said the vicar, the Reverend John Williams-Edwards, an engagingly rotund Pickwickian figure in

1 the Welsh congress of bards

2 a long-buttoned cassock

a diminutive pork-pie hat. 'You will sit at the back to observe the way we conduct divine worship at Mold Parish Church.'

It was a relief. I'd had more than enough of it for one day. I had just finished unpacking when he was back.

'One of our parochial layreaders is indisposed,' he said. 'I must require you to take Evensong at our daughter church of St James. Do you have a sermon appropriate to Trinity Sunday?'

I had indeed prepared such a discourse, an appraisal of the Trinitarian theology of the Cappadocian Fathers of the east compared to that promulgated in the west by the incomparable St Augustine of Hippo. The vicar gave me a lift in his car, dumped me outside the little church and drove off.

A tiny insistent bell was clanging as I entered the building, which was small, ordinary and brick built. It was unnerving. Never before had I conducted a service. Never before had I delivered a sermon. I had written sermons, certainly, but I had never stood up in a pulpit to hold forth. That, it transpired, was the least of my problems.

'Come this way,' said the churchwarden, a busy energetic man called Frank.

I was in the vestry, robed and ready, expecting to commence operations in cassock, surplice, scarf, and hood. He took me instead through a door out the back, along a narrow pathway behind the terraced Coronation Street houses till we came to a little wooden hall. Inside was a motley collection of children, one of them, I remember, got up as Bugs Bunny. Each was furnished with either a basket of eggs or a voluminous bunch of flowers. Nothing could have been more unexpected. Oblivious of Trinity Sunday, this was the annual Church of St James, New Brighton, 'Egg and Flower Service', the only congregation in the world, I think, to acknowledge the festival.

I hardly had time to think about it when, to a disjointed 'All things bright and beautiful', we braved the traffic in precarious procession along the busy main road. Somehow, we survived to enter the crowded church, standing room only. I knew it immediately. They would not be enthralled by the Cappadocian Fathers or the sublime, illustrious, supreme Doctor of the Church.

'Who was that St Disgusting you were on about?'

I went into the vestry while Frank was reading the lesson. I made a dot on a large piece of paper. When it came to the sermon, I held it up.

'What do you see?'

'A dot.'

'But what about all the white?'

The import was clear. They must look for the good in people, the white, instead of picking on their faults. Afterwards, I was crowded about with greetings and congratulations. At the church of St James after that I never looked back.

And so, at last I was launched. I was expected at the vicarage at nine the following morning, passing below the splendid parish church of St Mary the Virgin, which sits high on the mound that oversees the town. I already knew something of it, an object of our studies in architecture while I was at the school. We had visited the building, but most of the work was done in the classroom. It was a familiar sight nevertheless, though there was now a further dimension to it. I paused at the bottom of the steps to look up. It was difficult to believe. This, the very apogee of late mediaeval art, with its broad flattened arches and iridescent facades of glass, was to be my workplace. My reaction was fanciful rather than scholarly. It was like being confronted with a splendid old lady in her lace ever more petulant and unsurpassed with the passage of the years. I looked forwards to making her further acquaintance.

Everything had changed. Yet, no less equally, nothing had changed. I looked down the street towards the centre of town, evoking memories from my teenage years . . . those succulent pasties from Huskins, the butchers, that amplified my school dinners. I was interminably hungry in those days. Then there was Woolies halfway down on the left, purveyors of Monkey Brand Soap and Dr Williams' Pink Pills for Pale People. Somebody must have bought them.

Most main streets in North Wales are narrow. But these are wide, allowing for strings of busy market stalls on a Wednesday, at which anything and everything is sold. Nylon stockings were in short supply in those years of rationing after the war, but the street traders had them. A pretty fifth-form redhead from the school was offered a pair free if she would allow the leering stall holder to help her put them on. It caused much scurrilous excitement among her friends. I looked nostalgically down the street. There was so very much to remember.

The vicarage was approached by a dank, sunless driveway menaced by lofty buildings in an advanced state of decay, an imposing brick-built Georgian pile no less architecturally significant but of a quite different mindset from the church. It could not have been more inhospitable, characterised by ranks of tall, identical windows affording not the slightest hint of the interior. Nor was my sense of rebuttal lessened when the vicar ushered me into his study to the right of the front door, a box-like, featureless room, cluttered on every surface with stacks of disorderly papers.

'This,' he announced, 'is my lost-leaf filing system.' He seemed disproportionately elephantine in the midst of it. He allowed me not even the merest of smiles. 'Though let me assure you, Mr Hughes, all is not lost.'

I should probably have laughed, but I was no longer certain what to make of him. He shifted a pile and motioned me into a chair, discarding his informality as we got down to business. There was an intensity and a determination to him that belied my earlier impressions. He had read Welsh at university, yet his voice was urbanely English.

'I expect you to purchase an appropriate aide-memoire,' he said. He brought out a chunky blue, leather-bound pocket diary, bristling with papers. 'I commend *The Parson's Pocketbook*. It's not inexpensive, but it contains information invaluable to the clergy. I would not be without it.' His fingers tapped the cover. 'I must forewarn you. The lessons appointed to be read are for use by the clergy of the Church of England. You will need a lectionary of the Church in Wales.'[3]

He leaned forwards, examining my reactions.

'At your theological college you were instructed in the prerequisites of the faith. It is my responsibility to see them put to practical effect. We will therefore begin by fulfilling the requirements of *The Book of Common Prayer.* As members of the clergy we are obligated to say the Daily Office. Therefore, as from tomorrow, you will join me on weekdays every morning at eight to read Morning Prayer in the parish church.'

There was no way I could argue with that. His commitment was indisputable. Unlike many of the clergy, there was no ethereal or otherworldly quality to him.

He continued, 'Now to matters mundane. I have spoken to Neville Bithell, our parish treasurer. You will be paid nine pounds, ten shillings a week, the money to be disbursed quarterly.' He studied his diary. 'Since you will not have served a full quarter on the first of July, the initial payment of your stipend will be on the first of October.'

I found it difficult to believe. It was disheartening enough to know I was to receive so little. But that I was to be paid a parsimonious four times a year!

'I can't survive on that,' I said. 'There's no way I can manage without money for so long.'

3 The church was disendowed and disestablished under *The Welsh Church Act 1914.*

He seemed doubtful, no more forthcoming, I thought, than the intransigent vicarage in which he lived.

'I suppose we might consider affording you a small loan. I will discuss it with Mr Bithell.'

I was about to remonstrate further, but he cut me off.

'No, you will leave it to me.'

We moved on. As a deacon I could not pronounce Absolution or celebrate the Holy Communion, but there was a great deal I was expected to understand. It would, it emerged, have been edifying had I sat at the back of St Mary's the previous evening because there were distinct differences between the solemn enactment of divine service at Mold Parish Church and the unmitigated Egg and Flower festivities at her daughter church of St James.

'I don't suppose you will have taken part in a properly conducted Evensong,' the vicar said.

The concept had never occurred to me.

'I haven't taken part in very much of anything,' I replied. 'A few of the students went to help in the short-staffed churches of Cardiff. But I never did.'

I had not expected so intense an interest in Evensong, not the most elevating of the services of the church. An idea occurred to me. I thought it might lighten the proceedings.

'It doesn't mean I've not experienced many different types of services,' I said. 'While I was as at St Michael's, I took my evangelical friend William to the Maundy Thursday Tenebrae, Psalms and Responsories at the Anglo-Catholic church of St Martin's, Roath. The rite was beautiful and extraordinary. You should have heard his objections to it afterwards.' My voice deepened, recalling Will's endemic ineptitude, '"The monotone was monotonous."'

There was an abrupt irritation to the vicar's voice as he said, 'I meant a properly conducted Evensong, not some ridiculous proscribed ceremony of the high church.'

And so I was presented with the solemn business of the liturgy as it was conducted in Mold Parish Church, of a quite different provenance from the flamboyant Latin masses for which St Mary's was conceived.

'*The Book of Common Prayer* is the bedrock of our faith,' the vicar said, 'to which has accrued a wonderful heritage of church music dating back to the sixteenth century with the works of Tallis and Byrd. It is a tradition to which we do our utmost to subscribe.'

I could see it was different, rebutting Puritan iconoclasm with the elaborate style and culture of the Elizabethan court. He leaned forwards and touched my arm.

'I will therefore require you to take singing lessons. Few churches can afford so great a correlation with the past. St Mary's, as we have it, dates back to the 1490s, founded by the benefaction of Lady Margaret Beaufort, in the aftermath of his victory on Bosworth Field to mark her son Henry's[4] accession to the English throne.'

I had thought St Mary's exquisite, but there was a great deal more to it than that, embracing at a stroke the accession

4 Henry VII

of the Tudors, the hegemony of King Henry VIII and the multitudinous consequences of the English Reformation.

'Our church is of royal patronage,' he continued, 'permitting our choir to be robed in scarlet. To that we respond Sunday by Sunday as our choristers sing Morning and Evening Prayer.'

I had my reservations about it as I returned to the flat, but it was the pressing problem of money that primarily clouded my mind. Is that how the church treats its footsoldiers? Is not a man worthy of his hire? The labourers in the vineyard had their pay rounded up, not down.[5] I was already overdrawn at the bank. It was pernicious enough that I was to receive so little. It was worse that I was to be without any money at all for four months. How did he expect me to buy *The Parson's Pocketbook* . . . and pay for singing lessons? It quite beggared belief.

5 Matthew, 20, 10

CHAPTER 2

Here beginneth the lesson

It could not be ignored. I must acquire money from somewhere. But where? The more I thought about it, the more pressing the matter became. I needed at least enough to buy food. And what about the future? Had I come this far only to be rebuffed? And why was he talking about a loan? The money was mine on whatever date it was paid. It gave rise to a further question. Was I committed to serving this curacy? We live in a free country. Could I not simply tender my resignation, putting an end to the charade before it had hardly begun? It seemed a shame after all that training, but what else was I to do? Perhaps I should make an appeal to the bishop? A more practical solution came to mind. I could disobey the vicar. It raised a further question. I had sworn due and canonical obedience to the bishop and his successors 'in all things lawful', but he could not command me to jump in the river. Nor need I defer my every decision to the reactionary vicar of Mold.

The treasurer, Mr Bithell, I knew, was one of the partners at Bingham Price, a company of chartered surveyors and estate agents with offices on Chester Street in the centre of town. The girl at reception seemed unduly excited to see me.

'I will find out if he's free.' Her eyes sparkled. 'How am I to announce you?'

Within moments I was ushered in to a tall, balding man who smiled, rose and extended a hand.

'A warm welcome to the parish of Mold, Mr Hughes. I hope you will be very happy here. It's always good to see a new curate in the town.'

I explained my predicament. He laughed.

'You think it's unreasonable? You're not the only one. The last curate left within a week, but I wouldn't be too hasty if I were you. It takes time to get to know our vicar.'

He fussed around to find me a chair.

'The clergy in my experience are not always easy to understand,' he said. 'The vicar is often quite sensible. But he can be bloody minded when he puts his mind to it.' He waved a finger. 'I'll tell you one thing. He expects his curates to be prepared for any eventuality. Show the slightest hesitancy and you will be in the mire. Did he forewarn you about the eggs and flowers at New Brighton?'

I shook my head.

'Typical. Will it be alright if we pay you monthly?'

I nodded.

'But why did he tell me that I was to be paid quarterly?'

The girl reappeared with coffee and biscuits on a tray. Again, she seemed flustered. He waved a hand as she left.

'Take no notice of our Rosie. She's a promising trainee receptionist, but she becomes rather predatory when there's a new curate on the premises.'

I had thought St Mary's beautiful. The interior was no less exhilarating, managing a breath-taking equilibrium between intimations of untrammelled space and a no lesser perception of massive solidity. How could an accumulation of stone, glass and wood be assembled to make a man's thoughts turn to God? You might think it impossible. Yet it was achieved effortlessly at St Mary's, the impact heightened as the vicar and I took part in our first Morning Prayer:

> *Thou deckest thyself with light as it were with a garment: and spreadest out the heavens like a curtain.*
>
> *Who layeth the beams of his chambers in the waters: and maketh the clouds his chariot, and walketh upon the wings of the wind.*

Translated by Miles Coverdale in 1535, rhythmically superb, it anticipated the elegance of The Authorised Version of 1611.

Afterwards, I arranged an afternoon meeting with Mr Jason, the verger.

'I show people round all the time,' he said.

It could hardly have been more unsatisfactory. He indicated a jumble of fragmented stained glass in the window east of the main door.

'Them Roundheads smashed up that glass,' he said. He indicated a metal ring set into a stone slab in the floor. 'And that's where Cromwell tethered 'is 'orse.'[6]

I rang my lovely Ann that evening from the telephone kiosk at the base of the Bailey Hill, around the corner from my flat. I had some difficulty in getting through and was surprised to find myself chatted up by the operator. (Was she honing her feminine wiles? Is there such a thing as a feminine wile?) 'It's been a pleasure talking to you,' she said finally. 'You're through to Saltburn by the Sea. I wish you good luck with your curating.' Entranced as I was with the deep pools of her eyes and the taunting curve to her lips, a couple of clicks later I was talking to my delightful Ann in faraway Yorkshire where she was a teacher at a girls' private school. I told her of my joust with the vicar. 'The parish treasurer has resolved the problem,' I said. 'But the vicar is difficult to understand. I've no idea why he should think it proper to pay me quarterly. Maybe it's a reversion to the days when curates were the surplus to requirement sons of the landed gentry.'

Ann was amused. 'The runts of the litter, not fit to do anything else,' she giggled.

The next few days were devoted to settling in. My flat, on the first floor above a series of doctors' surgeries, was part of a property belonging to Roger Parker, a much liked, much respected retired GP, currently High Sheriff of Flintshire.

6 access to a junction in the Victorian bell-pull system

For years he and his family had occupied the rooms above the surgeries, part of which had since become my flat. But following his wife's death and his retirement, Roger had moved into a stylish new house in the grounds converted from one of the barns. Now in his mid-eighties, marooned in a chair, crippled with arthritis to the point of incapacity, he was cared for by Mrs Joan Wright, his housekeeper, who owned a scruffy white poodle called Mischief. She, I thought, was his primary problem, a rough and ready woman that only just kept the place clean. But Roger's domestic arrangements were not my responsibility. Nor did they impinge on our relationship. Since I had no television and we both liked Cliff Michelmore's *Tonight*, I usually dropped in to see him in the early evening.

Above all I wanted to make the best of my flat. If Ann and I were to be married, this would be our home. There was a great deal to be said for it, high-ceilinged, capacious, fully furnished including, to my astonishment, an upright Bechstein piano in the drawing room. I played a few notes. The sound was resonant, superb. There was a convenient little kitchen. There were plenty of shelves for my books. On the Wednesday, at my mother's insistence, I went to a nearby shop where I put up a notice advertising for a cleaner. My father had an antique Ford 8, bought second hand in 1936, which he had welded by the local blacksmith. The car was on its last legs, and he did not like bringing it into town. So, my mother came in by bus, did her shopping in the market, then dropped in for a coffee with me.

'The place needs a thorough cleaning once a week,' she said.

The problem was resolved that evening when I was visited by a bustling little woman called Ginny, to whom was annexed her perplexing, cloth-capped husband Fred. I found him extraordinary. I spoke to him. I received no reply. He sat in a chair, defiant, mindlessly layabout, evocative of the *Daily Mirror*'s Andy Capp.

I was in St Mary's each morning to say the Daily Office. Evensong I read for myself. But there was no denying the vicar. At Mattins on the following Sunday, I was relegated to the back in one of the pews under the organ gallery.

'You must read, mark, learn and inwardly digest,' he said.

It was interesting, nevertheless. There were commemorative plaques on the wall, one in memory of the Reverend William Wynne, Doctor of Divinity, Rector of Llanfechain in Montgomeryshire, a man of evidently strong opinions. To register his objections to what he considered to be the insanitary practice of allowing burials within the walls of the church, he arranged for his memorial to be instated during his lifetime. A further inscription marked his date of death, 17th March 1775. And then? It was all in vain. As part of the restorations of 1856, the architect, Sir George Gilbert Scott, had the apse built over him.

But there was no denying the resonance of the moment, the words and the music from many sources blended harmoniously, soaring as the chorister voices reached for the skies singing Ralph Vaughan Williams' 'O taste and see'. I was not normally an enthusiast for Mattins, but I was impressed. The vicar intoned the responses in a mellifluous tenor. I wondered if I could ever match him.

As at New Brighton, people gathered round to welcome me after the service. There was no doubting it. I had suddenly become a public figure. They would know me. I could not possibly remember them. Afterwards, I talked to the organist.

'Why don't you have girls in your choir?' I asked.

'Because the boys would not sing. They're lazy little devils. You can rely on girls. They will always sing . . . which gives the boys an excuse not to.' He shrugged his shoulders. 'But girls cannot project the same pure clarity of tone. You get a truly wonderful sound from boys.'

CHAPTER 3

The noose tightens . . .

There was more to be negotiated with the vicar at our meeting the following morning, in the event a great deal more. No sooner had we begun than he was back to the question of the liturgy. There was no disputing his conviction. I was tempted to confront him.

'The music at St Mary's is quite lovely,' I said. 'But it's performed on our behalf. Do you think that is right? My father detests the idea that a choir be allowed to overtake the efforts of the congregation, insisting above all that people be allowed to express the praises of God for themselves. They sing quite dreadful hymns in his church. It doesn't seem to matter. People embrace the moment, telling him how much they enjoyed the service.' His fingers drummed the desk. Evidently, I was trying his patience. 'It may not be aesthetically satisfying,' I said. 'But it means a great deal to them.'

There seemed no point in prevaricating. I looked him in the eye. 'Nor is a lack of quality thought to be an impediment elsewhere. There are hymns sung in all the churches. How many of them could be included in a literary anthology? You might find Blake's "Jerusalem" and probably something from Cowper. But for all her popularity no self-respecting editor would endorse the lyrics of Mrs Alexander."[7] He seemed quite unmoved. Had I overstepped the mark? There was nothing else for it. I attempted to amuse him.

'Nor should we necessarily put our trust in literary talent. By the pen of Joseph Addison, no less, "thy rod and thy staff comfort me" is demoted to a "friendly crook",[8] reminiscent of Flash Harry in *The Belles of St Trinian's*.'

The vicar afforded me a steady glare. Perhaps he had yet to see the movie. It was time to change tack.

'The lecturers at the theological college were not enamoured of *The Book of Common Prayer*,' I said, 'finding the services tedious, wordy, cobbled together in 1662[9] to meet the exigencies of the day.'

He nodded. It seemed to mollify him.

'They are mistaken,' he replied. 'The services of *The Book of Common Prayer* were brought into being on the principle that an artist puts together a collage, plagiarising materials from the past to create a new and distinctive work of art.'

7 Mrs Cecil Frances Alexander, 1818–95, prolific Anglo-Irish hymnologist, author of 'All things bright and beautiful' and 'Once in royal David's city'

8 *Though in the paths of death I tread,*
With gloomy horrors overspread.
My steadfast heart shall fear no ill.
For Thou, O Lord, art with me still.
Thy friendly crook shall give me aid
And guide me through the dreadful shade.

9 reintroduced in 1662 after the Restoration of the Monarchy

He rose to collect an Everyman edition from the bookshelves, flicking through the pages.

'This is a facsimile copy of *The Book of Common Prayer* put out in 1549, our first prayer book in the vernacular after more than a thousand years of Latin. The contents were written by others, but it remains an act of collage-making at the hand of the martyred archbishop.'[10] His finger prodded the page. 'Nor should we think it right to usurp its elegance. "'O Lord, open thou our lips, And our mouth shall show forth thy praise . . ."'

He gave me something of a glare.

'What is a praise? A psalm is a praise. Therefore, we sing the psalms.' He became quite intense. 'That much can be said for the language. Nor does the music prove any less a matter of consequence. The Greek word "*psalmoi*" means "instrumental music", allowing for the psalms to be accompanied by trumpets, lutes and harps, cymbals and dances. As you know, the structure of Hebrew poetry is quite different from our own, a rhyming of thoughts rather than of words. So people began to transmute the psalms into verse. The best known is the twenty-third set to the tune "Crimond".'

He raised a finger.

'But unique to the Church of England and therefore to us there emerged the mode of psalm singing known as the Anglican Chant. No doubt it is done less well in your

10 Archbishop Cranmer was burnt at the stake in Oxford, 21st March 1556.

father's church. Properly sung it is in every way appropriate when the psalms are sung in more reputable establishments. Their impact is inimitable. You only have to listen to the choral Evensongs put out daily by the BBC.' He bowed his head. 'Nor do we do at all badly in that respect when our parish choir sings the psalms.'

It evidently meant a great deal to him. My objections were not wholly serious. I found it irresistible, nevertheless.

'The application of music can be quite potty,' I said. '*The Cathedral Prayer Book* has a fully scored edition of "The Churching of Women" where one of the postpartum mothers is expected to sing bass. How on earth can she be expected do that?'

He nodded. To my surprise it amused him, for the first time eliciting the miniscule glimmer of a smile.

'Sir John Stainer expected the ladies to be accompanied by a choir,' I said. 'But it would be quite inappropriate. The people of the Old Testament believed that the act of procreation is a sin for which a woman requires absolution. At least I think that's what they thought. They didn't go in for purifying the man. But there's no sense of penance to "The Churching of Women". It's an act of thanksgiving to rejoice at the birth of a child. You wouldn't lay on bells and whistles for that.'

He evidently agreed.

'We should get back to the point,' he said. 'I know there are different ways of expressing the faith. But at our parish church of St Mary the Virgin we are committed to the traditional services of the church, not only Morning and

Evening Prayer but on the first Sunday of each month with a full choral celebration of the Holy Communion.'

I gave it further consideration as I went away, accentuating the essential differences between us. My convictions were conventional enough, reflecting the principles advocated at the theological college. It was quite striking. The great mediaeval establishment of St Mary's may have embodied history, but the present order of services at Mold Parish Church was definitively out of date. The vicar had stressed the importance of Morning and Evening Prayer, but nobody at the theological college would dispute the idea that the Sacrament was infinitely more important than the speaking of the Word. What was done at the altar was of far greater significance than what was expressed within the chancel or in the pews. At St Michael's it was a *sine qua non*. The Holy Eucharist was the primary and central service of the day. Yet at Mold Parish Church, on three Sundays out of four, the Holy Communion was relegated to a said celebration at eight.

One thing was evident. There was nothing I could do about it. I had always regarded myself as belonging to a new era, destined to rectify the deleterious practices of the past, but a newly ordained deacon cannot expect to demand change. The vicar had spoken of the efficacy of the words and the music and with that I concurred, but he was also mistaken. Not the finest of words nor the most enthralling of music can give expression to the unalloyed mysteries of God. It remains to the enigma of the eucharist to do that.

Yet nowhere was it acknowledged here. Nor was there a way I could circumvent it. That was the impasse. I had signed the bishop's ledger. The legislators must have their way. Not only did they outlaw adultery but, *force majeure*, I was licensed to serve my title in the refractory parish of Mold.

I talked to Ann about it later over the phone. I knew exactly what to expect.

'I've never understood why you're wasting your life on the church,' she said. 'Everybody knows you could do better.'

It was a bone of contention between us, though I was not sure what was meant by better. It seemed ridiculous. She wanted us to run a pub.

'You're a member of an old-fashioned and very strange profession,' she said, 'surrounded by absurd conventions. I know you say it's not etiquette. But why on earth should people not address you as Reverend?[11] It doesn't make sense.'

I could think of no answer to that.

'I'll tell you one thing,' I said. 'I've not made a good start. It was entirely my fault. The vicar probably thought me a twit. We got at cross purposes when I tried to make him laugh.' I could hear her giggling at the other end. 'There were times when I think I really annoyed him. He didn't even smile when I mentioned Addison's "friendly crook".'

I detected no small an element of mischief in her voice. 'Did you mention that hymn where "all the virgins bare their parts"?'

11 The clergy are addressed as Mr, except on envelopes.

It was one of her favourite jokes:

Our Lady sings Magnificat
With tune surpassing sweet;
And all the Virgins bear their parts,
Sitting about her feet.

That would be altogether a step too far.

CHAPTER 4

Cilcain

There was a point advocated at the theological college. I had always found it strange. The lecturers were forever urging us to ethereal and otherworldly thoughts. Yet they were adamant that days off were of the utmost importance to members of the clergy, not to be neglected or overlooked. I had disregarded the idea for weeks, but persistently it came back to haunt me. Perhaps it really was a failure on my part. So finally, I relented, took a day off and went home.

An ear-splitting racket and a sizzle of steam greeted me as I arrived in the village. Evan Jones, the blacksmith, was at the forge, hammering a horseshoe into shape. I wondered how he went about riveting my father's car. He was never at work in the early morning, allowing us to play an unruly game of football in the square as we waited for the school bus. The village was tranquil as I walked up the road and through the churchyard on the way to the house. The long Georgian cream-clad vicarage was bathed in sunshine as I arrived, evoking memories from my teenage years, the big open lawn where we played French cricket, the developing crop of cooking apples on the other side of the hedge. The red squirrels were there. Our cat used to catch them, alerting us to each kill by leaving its tail on the doormat.

I was twelve when we moved to Cilcain. I remembered our preliminary visit when my father was offered the incumbency. My mother hated the house – there was not a room, corridor or lavatory that was not decorated purple, the previous incumbent's wife having been passing through the purple period of her life. But my father had gone into rhapsodies over the church.

There were so many memories as I went, so much to recall. There was the girl called Rosemary, the very first love of my life. We were both thirteen. She was clever and pretty with deep soulful eyes. I meant as much to her as she did to me. I was stupid when I broke it off. I felt I had to for the sake of the rest of my life. But it was cruel and I was wrong. I had never stopped regretting it.

Then there was my first experience of the Parochial Church Council. My father, also Richard, was an awkward man, an unruly crumbled figure who somehow had managed to live two lives. In the first I could imagine him, a proud, upright young soldier from a Welsh village, wet behind the ears, plunged into the deadly maelstrom of the Somme. His brother was killed. He was wounded. Also he was deafened by the incessant thunder of the guns. He would never be the same. And then? He became headmaster of a village primary school. But he felt more of him was required. So, a confirmed bachelor, he saved and scrimped the money to pay for his tuition at the theological college in Lichfield.

His second life began sometime after his fortieth birthday when he married my mother, Mary. She was a lowland Scot. I was the eldest of their four children. It was claustrophobic. Redolent of the patriarch Abraham, it was my father's dearest wish that, like the ram of Azazel,[12] his eldest son be offered up for ordination. So, at the age of eighteen, by way of a preliminary, I was made a member of the Parochial Church Council. Nothing will eliminate the memory of that first meeting. An old man called Jim Hanborough stood up soon after the start. I had always rather liked him, but he made a long speech condemning everything my father had done. According to Hanborough, never was there an incumbent so utterly neglectful of his responsibilities.

'All he wants is money,' he said. 'He doesn't care about anything else.'

He raged on about it interminably, further turning the screw. So what happened next? My father turned to my mother, leaning forwards. There was a rasping quality to his voice when he said, 'What did he say?' But he wasn't as deaf as all that.

I let myself in. Nothing much was happening at home. My sisters and my younger brother were at school. As my mother always said, 'We have a proper meal in the evening. I lay on a snack in the middle of the day.' We had salad with tomatoes and boiled ham. It was predictable. My mother

12 the scapegoat released into the wilderness, Leviticus 16, 6–10

was a quiet woman. It took the impact of an absurd decor to rouse her, though she had not taken to Ann.

We talked about this and that. My father had pressing problems of his own, though these were nothing new. His predecessor, the Reverend John Wilkinson, husband to her of the purple walls, had been advised of an infestation of the death watch beetle in the roof of the church. He arranged for its disinfestation and repair. Then, abruptly, he changed parish, leaving his successor to foot the bill. It was the priority of my father's life. Endlessly he organised lists of subscribers, sales of work, coffee mornings and jumble sales. But it was like climbing Everest. A painted thermometer was put up outside the church,marking the progress of the fundraising. It had not changed in months. A further four thousand pounds invariably were required.

I left in the late afternoon and looked in at the church, unusual in that it had two equal aisles. But it was the south aisle that mattered, overhung with a late mediaeval roof of mellowed oak hammerbeams culminating in eight large decorative seraphs at the end of each terminal. It was one of the treasures of Wales, adding to my father's woes.

People think craftsmen of the past were not so skilled as those of the present. Visitors to the church were told that, after its dissolution in 1555, the hammerbeam roof at Cilcain was salvaged from among the remains of the refectory at Basingwerk Abbey, near Holywell. Some people believed it. Somebody I was told had tried to track its itinerary from farm to farm. But the positioning of each hand-cut joist was unique. It would be impossible to reassemble. The primitive panels and the pale ochre of the timbers suggests that its origins were indigenous, fashioned *in situ* by the local craftsmen of the day.

CHAPTER 5

The host of midian . . .

I had not been in Mold long before I discovered that on Friday evenings the streets were inundated with Teddy Boys. There was some sort of collusion between them because on weeknights they could be found in other North Wales towns, Buckley, Holywell, Denbigh and the like. The style, I was told, originated with the tailors of Saville Row attempting to revive an Edwardian dandy culture to counter the austerities of post-war Britain. It had become *de rigueur* among the young and wealthy of the home counties. But the style did not catch on without acquiring further characteristics of its own, a token of rebellious youth in league with the rise of American rock 'n roll, unique to Britain nevertheless, finding expression in tapered trousers, knee-length jackets, elaborately embroidered waistcoats and monster clomping brothel-creeper shoes, the whole ensemble crowned with an Elvis-style coiffure designated a DA[13]. No longer Edwardian, they were nevertheless labelled Teddy Boys when in 1953 a headline in the *Daily Express* abridged *Edwardian*

13 a duck's arse

to *Teddy*. For all that, they puzzled me. How could they afford so extravagant a gear?

At first, I found them difficult to understand. Were they simply on a fashion parade? Initially they seemed innocuous enough. Then I began to hear of their vandalising of telephone kiosks and the fights they provoked outside pubs and dance halls. They finally attained notoriety when a contingent visited the ladies' public lavatories in the town, smothering the seats in a copious layer of sticky brown paint. I could see why they might find it arousing. But shrouded in the flouncy skirts of the day, there was no way they could observe the indelicate fruits of their crime. Nor, except by hanging around outside, could they identify the ladies they thus had dignified with the mark of Cain,[14] though on second thought that was probably a tattoo.

But it was done at a price. They probably shoplifted the paint, but to achieve entrance to each of the cubicles they need, must spend a penny. It was an earnest topic of conversation, I discovered, among the old ladies of the town.

I told Ann about the Teds. She was amused, certainly. But predictably, there was a sting in the tail.

'You should show them more understanding,' she said. 'I know they should not have painted the lavatory seats. It must have been an absolute pig to get off. But you're a man of the cloth. It's your job to forgive "the sinful lusts of the flesh".'

14 Genesis 4, 15

She was hardly a churchgoer. I wondered how she could cite *The Book of Common Prayer*. But she was right. There was no questioning it. The French word for 'vicar' is '*curé*', so that vicariously the clergy were universally expected to cure the many sins of the world. So, I wondered, should I attempt to convert the Teddy Boys? It hardly seemed practicable. The remit was one thing, the reality another.

What then, if anything, had been achieved during my brief time as curate? Nothing very much, it seemed. A little quick thinking had salvaged my sermon at New Brighton. It was hardly theologically profound. Nor had I excelled during my contacts with the vicar. One thing was evident. There could not be a greater disparity between the two long preparatory years of my training and the practical realities that confronted me as I took up my title as the assistant curate of Mold.

CHAPTER 6

Just as I am . . .

There was no doubt about it. I almost regretted it. My training seemed virtually irrelevant. Llandaff Cathedral and the nearby theological college of St Michael and All Angels were bombed to near destruction by the Luftwaffe during the war. But at the time of my arrival in the autumn of 1955, while the cathedral remained to be reconsecrated,[15] the college was returned to practically new condition, given a degree of panache as the flamboyant reds and golds of the dining hall's ceiling caused the occupants of passing cars to mistake us for a night club. The regime within was forbiddingly austere nevertheless, semi-monastic. Each morning began with two hours in the college chapel allowing for Mattins and a Eucharist, followed by a protracted period of silent contemplative prayer. That in particular I had found irksome. I could not pray subject to the dictat of the clock. We wore black cassocks as we went about the business of the day and inhabited a domain apart, given to one stern principle. At all times we had to eschew any 'occasion for sin'.

15 On 6th August 1960, in the presence of Queen Elizabeth II, Epstein's *Majestas* was in place for the reconsecration of the nave.

But there was no such austere perfectionism to my life as I began my travails as the assistant curate of Mold. The college had disciplined me. Now I must regulate myself. It was going to be difficult. I had never been a model student from the start. The truth cannot be gainsaid. I found the college invasive, stifling, obliging me from time to time to make my escape. One of my friends possessed a seventy-eight of *The Bewitching Miss Bassey* which we played repeatedly, in which she went about burning her candle at both ends.

It was the jaunty little tune that did it, that and her tiny hesitation, hanging momentarily in the air before culminating explicitly 'at both ends'. On many an absentee afternoon we revelled in the wilful voice of the young lady from Splott . . . though they called it Tiger Bay, which sounded better.

So I began to come to terms with it. I would never be a saintly à Kempis[16] or a St John of the Cross.[17] But I was determined to make of it what I could. I had never thought of myself as a public speaker, yet I knew more or less what was required when it came to Evensong at the daughter church of St James and in the old school at Gwernymynydd. I had always thought sermons uninteresting, my father's in particular, so I told the congregation stories which, it

16 c 1380–1472, German-Dutch theologian, author of *The Imitation of Christ*

17 1542–91, Spanish mystic and Carmelite friar

seemed, they liked. They had never heard of the ill-fated love affair of Abelard[18] and Heloise, or the strange ascetic life of St Simeon Stylites.[19] At St Mary's, on the other hand, the vicar monitored my every move. At first, I was expected simply to observe and to learn. Then, after some rehearsal, I was permitted to take my place in the chancel where I read the prayers. From time to time, I was required to attend and take note as he conducted the occasional services of the church. Weddings, I discovered, required particular attention, with rehearsals beforehand and banns to be read.

'I was once responsible,' the vicar said, 'for a wedding where the bridegroom gave me a false name. He thought he could escape his responsibilities. But the clergy are not accountable when they are told lies.' He gave a satisfied smile. 'That is why the witnesses are important. No matter what he called himself, he had made his vows publicly, "before God and this company".'

There were times when I wondered whether I should be serving my curacy elsewhere. There was no doubt about it. I felt left behind. Mold was a bit of a backwater. We had been at the Alyn School together, but most of my friends had moved away to take up exciting and well-paid jobs. One of them had joined the RAF and was flying jets along the

18 1079–1142, scholastic philosopher, poet and musician. His tragic love affair with Heloise culminated in his castration.

19 He spent thirty-seven years of the fifth century on the top of a pillar near Aleppo.

borders of the Soviet Union, by a directive of the government violating their airspace to antagonise the Russians. It was dangerous. It was tendentious. He laughed and called it a 'pinprick of the cold war'. The contrast between us could not have been greater. He was swanning around in a silver-grey Sunbeam Alpine, while I had yet to take my driving test. Meanwhile, another of my friends was beginning to write for the BBC. My vocation was important – I had no wish to abandon my ministry – but I was tempted by adverts in *The Church Times* offering exotic curacies in places such as Oxford or Ely. It was a delusion as before. I had signed the bishop's ledger. I tried to console myself. Talent can be found in the most unexpected places.

My father was brought up in Llanystumdwy in south Caernarfonshire, a generation later but of the same village as David Lloyd George who had become their local MP. Uniquely, for a man who had risen to high office in Westminster, his first language was not English but Welsh. My father told me of a meeting in the village hall sometime before 1916 when Lloyd George was Chancellor of the Exchequer. I could envisage him ensconced on the stage, a volatile, formidable figure, ready to take the questions of his constituents, mostly villagers and tenant farmers.

'Mister Chancellor. There's farm labourer here that wants to ask you a question.' 'Oh,' said the Chancellor, 'bring him forwards. Let's have a look at him.'

They pushed the lad forwards, an awkward, ungainly figure. 'Begin by taking your hands out of your pockets.'

'At least they're in my pockets, Mr Chancellor.'[20]

It hit home like a rocket. The Chancellor found it as funny as everybody else. I was reminded of the lines in Grey's *Elegy:*

Full many a flow'r is born to blush unseen,
And waste its sweetness on the desert air.

I hoped it wasn't true of me.

20 *'Mistar Canghellor. Mae gwasc fferm yma sydd am ofyn cwestiwn i chi.'*
'O,' meddai'r Canghellor, 'dewch ag ef ymlaen. Gadewch i mi edrych arno.'
Fe wthnasant y bachgen ymlaen, ffigwr llechwith, trwsgl.
'I ddechreu, tynna dy ddwylo allan o dy bocedi.'
'O leiaf maent yn fy mhocedi i, Mistar Canghellor.'

CHAPTER 7

. . . Without one plea

So, my curacy went on. I had quizzed the organist, James Dickens, following that first Mattins at St Mary's. Now I got to know him, a diminutive wiry man with a pleasant manner who recently had joined the staff at the Alyn School. Unsurprisingly, he was from South Wales. Choir practice was held in St Mary's on Thursday and Friday evenings at six. We arranged to meet one evening at five thirty.

'The main difficulty,' he said, 'is the construct of the organ. By any measure a massive mistake on the part of the architect.'

He pulled out a few stops and ran his fingers over the keys. Above us, the pipes of the choir organ rang out. He pushed them in and pulled out others. There was a perceptible delay before there was a response from the great organ in the gallery against the west wall.

'You see? He could place ranks of pipes anywhere he liked, though I can't imagine how he induced Rushworth and Dreaper to install a tubular pneumatic action. It was definitively out of date even then. It's rough on the poor organist. I'm obliged to play the notes without listening to what I'm playing.'

He turned to me.

'But enough of my problems. The vicar wants me to help you with your singing.'

It was a relief. I had expected to pay for the tuition. And certainly, the lessons that followed were illuminating, eliciting unsuspected qualities from my distinctly unmusical voice. I could bring forth a natural vibrato. There was more to me than I thought.

A couple of Sundays later I sang the responses at Morning Prayer. Nobody noticed. Nobody said anything about my improved voice. But an altogether different matter engaged my attention. I had sensed something of them before. Now it was evident. The pews were stocked with ranks of fashionably turned out, exquisitely lipsticked young women. The vicar and I stood at the back to speak to the parishioners as they left. Neville Bithell put a cheerful hand on my shoulder.

'Our little Rosie's got competition,' he said. 'They're all after you now.' I was not sure I believed him.

But there swiftly arose another female reaction to my curacy. The one phenomenon seemed to follow from the other.

'It must be very awkward for you on a Sunday morning,' said Miss Elizabeth Jones, a diminutive grey woman with severely pinned-back hair, probably in her late-sixties, who regularly attended the Holy Communion at St Mary's at eight. 'Why don't you join me for breakfast after the service?'

It took me by surprise. Sunday mornings were not particularly different. I always tumbled out of bed at the last minute in time for church.

'It will be just like the old days,' she said. 'My late brother was vicar of Pontblyddyn. He was a bachelor. I was his housekeeper. So I made a point of seeing he had a proper breakfast on a Sunday morning. Do you prefer a boiled egg or something fried?' There was a curious immediacy to it.

'Are you expecting me today?'

'I don't see why not,' she said. 'I live on Earl Road, number thirty-four. Come when you can. I will have it ready for you.'

Sunday mornings were never the same after that. I did not think her particularly affluent, yet the breakfasts were a plenitude of bacon, eggs, marmalade and toast. It allowed her to berate practically everything that took place at the church. Mostly, she talked about the ineptitude of the vicar who, unlike her dear departed brother, had not an inkling of how a parish should be run. I did my best to exonerate him, to no great effect.

'Why he was made incumbent of Mold,' she said, is beyond me. All he does is gossip with his cronies. He doesn't give a single thought to the rest of us. Through her I came to know her friends, the skeletal, ivory-skinned Miss Georgina Prince and the bulkily formidable Mrs Joanna Wellesley-Davies, mistress of all she surveyed. I not only liked these old ladies but had penetrated something of their mystery. In concert with their more nubile counterparts, they too were given to fancying curates.

It was a strange phenomenon certainly, but of one thing I was certain. My dog collar was the reason for it. Women had never assiduously taken an interest in me before. Then one Wednesday morning when some friends of my mother's were coming to tea, I went down to the market to buy cups and saucers from one of the stalls on the High Street. It took some time. Finally, I came across some blue and white Royal Doulton seconds. The stall holder was a tall, frizzy-haired woman in grey overalls.

'You're the curate,' she said. 'My daughter Rosie is on about you the whole time. She's even taken to going to church.' The market was crowded, and she was interminably busy, but what she said was important. 'Rosie is at a lovely age. I remember going through my own teenage fantasy of love's young dream. The trouble is it can't last. A girl has to grow up.'

So that was it. The curate was Rosie's paradigm on her way through adolescence. I felt a surge of love for her at the thought of it. It was ridiculous, nevertheless. Who in her senses would want to marry a penniless parson? And the old ladies? Perhaps they had never entirely lost the urge.

Which brought me again to Ann, by far the most incomprehensible of the women I was expected to understand. But the weeks had flown by, and nothing could have been more magical than the moment when she descended from the bus that brought her to me from Birkenhead, as enchanting as ever, her insouciance, her determined awkwardness, her sheer physical beauty. Nobody could possibly quantify that. It was St Augustine who prayed, 'Give me chastity and abstinence, but not yet.'[21] I said not ever. Did that subvert the teachings of the New Testament? 'It is good for a man

21 *Confessions*, 8, 7

not to touch a woman,'[22] says the first epistle to the Corinthians, cutting off at a stroke the entire future of the human race. But Paul was a misogynist. He certainly didn't believe in the equality of the sexes.

Fortunately, the vicar harboured no such reservations. When he knew Ann was coming, he allowed us a week's holiday, which we dissipated with kisses and laughter on the banks of the Dee in Chester and at the Loggerheads trailing the meandering pathways of the Leete. In the interest of propriety, she was accommodated by Miss Georgina Prince. There was a hole in my heart when she left.

22 1 Corinthians 7, 1

CHAPTER 8

All good things around us . . .

So, I turned to lesser things. I was captivated by a marble colossus in the northwest corner of St Mary's commemorating 'Dr Robert Davies of Llanerch, Esq, 1684–1728'. It was extraordinary. It was perplexing. It required a little research. Not only was the deceased descended from the archetypal princes of Powys but, on his own part, was a distinguished antiquarian and collector of rare Welsh manuscripts. Yet surprisingly, in a period given to hyperbolic adulation of the deceased, none of this was recognised on his monument. Nor, for that matter, were we told where he was buried. The more I thought about it, the more I was intrigued.

The sculptor, it transpired, was Henry Cheere, later Sir Henry, though at the age of twenty-five he was but recently discharged from an apprenticeship. Then, by whatever means, he set up business in the grounds of St Margaret's Church within the curtilage of Westminster Abbey. The other principal figure was his widow, acknowledged in a separate inscription: 'At the cost of his wife Anne.'

A number of questions arose. Why did she requisition so extravagant a memorial? Cheere's part in it was there for all to see, not unexpectedly in an age obsessed with classical antiquity presenting us with an idealised heroic figure in a Roman '*toga virilis*'. Cheere's works are described in the textbooks as a combination of Palladian and Rococo, though this I found exclusively Rococo, frilly at the edges, flamboyant, audacious, a young man's work not entirely appropriate to funerary purposes. To mark the deceased's mastery of affairs, a globe of the world was fashioned to stand at his left elbow . . . which could not but be mistaken for a boiled egg. Had Cheere, in his youthful enthusiasm, created a folly? It was difficult to decide. Perhaps, indeed rightly, was the resultant sculpture known by all and sundry as 'the man with the egg'.

I tried to gauge Anne Davies' part in it. The price must have been excruciating coming from so auspicious a workshop, to which must be added Cheere's remuneration, the production of his sketches and plans for her approval, the quarrying and cost of the marble, the fees he charged for the service of his apprentices, the cartage, the hire of horses and hauliers, and their use of the turnpikes and staging inns as they traversed the potholed seventeenth century roads of the land. Nor was that all. Did Anne visit him at Westminster or was Cheere obliged to make the wearisome journey, perhaps several times, to Llanerch to attend on her there? That too must be added to the bill.

There was one further point to it. The separate inscription, 'at the cost of his wife Anne', was to be taken seriously. The daughter of John Brockholes, Esq, of Claughton Hall of Claughton in Lancashire,[23] would have money of her own. But why did she instate so ostentious a memorial? Was it a dynastic assertion of her hierarchical power? Or did it reflect her dedication to her husband's memory, a widow's poignancy following her consort's demise? The sculpture, I thought, amply reflected Cheere's youthful grandiosity, but what was to be made of her? She did not let us know. There was certainly no blazoning of her husband's achievements nor any evident expression of her grief, leaving me again to ponder the conundrum of the feminine mind.

There was a corollary to it, quite unexpected. When I came to read about it in Archdeacon Thomas' *A History of the Diocese of St Asaph*,[24] I found that the Robert Davies monument masks a sixteenth century decorative niche, one of two episcopal memorials within the building placed earlier in memory of Bishop Parfew.[25] The archivist had ousted the bishop. What was I to make of that? Archdeacon Thomas supplied the answer. Lady Margaret Beaufort was a doyenne of the late Middle Ages. She had set the precedent. There was an earlier church on the site which she swept peremptorily away. Nor, from what I imagined of her, was

23 c 1600

24 1874

25 in office, 1536–55

Anne Davies of Llanerch any less determined. Though they were long past, I could envisage them. Such great ladies were matriarchal, absolutely a law unto themselves.

My thoughts returned to Ann, my enthralling, dedicated mathematician and committed atheist, the ultimate dilemma of my life. It might not be consistent with my calling, but I loved her beyond measure. Never was there a more enchanting, more able, delectable, tantalising and thoroughly determined young woman. She was a law unto herself. I would not have it otherwise. But things had moved on since our days at the university. It had been part of our speculative chatter in the students' union. No longer did she have visions of our running a pub, nor was she sure she was willing to marry me. It was her predicament. How could we reconcile my faith with her absolutism? It was evident. Neither of us should have anything to do with the other.

CHAPTER 9

She didn't say no . . .

The answer was plain. I should abandon my dog collar. I was not prepared to do that. Nor could I bear the thought of losing that heart-searching, impish gleam in her eye, the wilful intransigence of her soul. There was one consolation to it. She might have her misgivings, but our unrelenting letters and phone calls made the point: she was no less engrossed with me than I was entranced by her.

She was busy during the summer holidays, helping out in Liverpool at her aunt's shop on New Scotland Road. They were forever being burgled. Absurdly, a policeman did nothing when he saw Ann chasing a robber up the street.

'He was making off with Aunty Lilly's cigarette vending machine,' she said. 'He'd ripped it off the wall. That half-baked rozzer could easily have caught him. It was an awkward thing to carry.' Then she saw the funny side of it. 'The burglar was asthmatic. He should give up burglary. He had a terrible cough.'

But my job was at a low ebb. The whole world was on holiday. I attended the Daily Office each morning and played my part in the Sunday services. I took over from Mr Jason whenever there was a tour of the church.

I wondered whether I should redecorate the flat. It did not seem particularly necessary, and I couldn't afford it. I did not expect to feel bereft at the absence of the vicar, but there was no ignoring it when there was a locum in the vicarage while he and his family went on holiday. He did not tell me where they were going.

'I will furnish you with a telephone number,' he said. 'On no account should you disclose it to anybody.'

What, I wondered, was the object of that?

There was nevertheless a significant development while they were away. I went over one evening to see Roger Parker, anticipating a sherry.

'No,' I replied when he asked me if I knew how to drive. 'I've not taken driving lessons, though I did have a go in my father's new Ford Popular.'

'A sit up and beg!' he said, clearly amused. 'Noisy little beggars. I've seen them about.' Suddenly he became serious. He took another pull at his cigarette. 'So why don't you learn to drive mine? It's in the garage.' He looked down at himself disconsolately. 'It's no longer of use to me. But I hold a valid license. I can be your qualified driver to accompany you. There's nothing in the Highway Code to stop us from doing that.'

It seemed incongruous, within the letter of the law if not compliant to the spirit of the law. In practical terms, there was no way he could rescue me were I to get into trouble. But we could not be prosecuted for that. The housekeeper found the keys and I went to inspect the car, a sturdy black

Hillman Snipe, smaller but identical in shape to the big Humbers of the funeral directors. The following day, I bought L plates and applied for a provisional license.

So my driving career began apace. The open road beckoned. We went out almost daily. It was probably hazardous, but one thing was apparent. Roger was so immeasurably bored he would rather jeopardise life and limb than remain in the house. Mrs Wright piled him into the front passenger seat while I stuck his wheelchair in the boot. Sometimes we were expected to take the poodle, Mischief . . . which required long periods of parking while Mrs Wright took the little menace for a walk. (Mischief had stolen a pound of raw sausages from my flat, bought only the previous week . . . which culminated in messes on Roger's carpets. It was embarrassing.)

Roger made not the slightest observations about my driving and offered no advice. The Snipe I found easy to handle. The column gear change presented no great difficulties, though the car shuddered volcanically when it was put into reverse.

And so the long days of summer faded gradually away, culminating on 25th August in the annual Bank Holiday Garden Fete at Mrs Fairburn-Willis' garden on Ruthin Road. She was a tall, thin and very well-organised woman.

'Call me Daphne,' she said when I went to see her.

It was amazing. The stallholders came from far and wide, though we hardly saw any of them in church. As had been done in previous years, the men laid a track for a miniature railway on which the children could ride around the grounds. I wanted to do something too, so I found a cudgel, a short piece of drainpipe and a stuffed woolly rat. It seemed an odd contribution, but it was the best I could do.

An ice cream van was parked in the driveway when I went up the evening before. The little train was hooting and trundling about. Daphne was in her element, directing people here and there. The house, I noticed, was hermetically sealed. Neville Bithell had put up notices. Admission was one shilling, but children were allowed in free.

The grounds were a hive of activity. There were several dogs on the loose. Men were putting up awnings while the women were arranging their stalls. For the most part I didn't know the people. But Joanna Wellesley-Davies was ensconced in a bower in the shrubbery . . . having anointed herself as the clairvoyant 'Mystic Molly'. She was no more mystical than a lamb chop. I wandered about. Old Charlie Williams, the vicar's warden, was about to hang up bunting. I offered to climb the ladder in his place. He was full of goodwill.

'Have you heard the weather forecast?' he asked. 'I hope it will be sunny tomorrow.'

It could not have been more satisfactory. There was hardly a cloud in the sky. People were in a festive mood, and the grounds were packed. Everywhere was heard the gratifying tinkle of cash.

'I will double your money,' I said, 'if you can hit the rat as it comes out of the drain.'

The fete was to receive the proceeds were the rodent to elude the participants. At the end of the afternoon, I had not made very much.

CHAPTER 10

Pastures new

Things were revving up with the end of the holidays. The Garden Fete signalled the change. It was quite exciting. I wanted to get going. There was a great sense of freedom to parish life. I decided to try my hand at parochial visiting. It was probably premature, so I did not mention it to the vicar.

Visiting had been strongly advocated at the theological college. 'The parson, "*the persona*", is to personify God's glory to the benefit of his people.' I found it absurd, a theological hyperbole. So, I decided to work it out for myself. *The Book of Common Prayer* uses the word 'indifferently', by which it means 'impartially', which perhaps seemed to provide the answer. Each dwelling, large or small, rich or poor, should be approached indifferently. If I was told to go away, I should leave forthwith. Were I invited in, I should do so. I wasn't looking to achieve any sort of benefit, as though I were some kind of holy salesman on the part of the church. My aim was to emulate Chaucer's *povre persoun:*

He was a shepherde and noght a mercenarie.
And thogh he hooly were and vertuous,

He was to synful men nat despitous,
Ne of his speche daungerous ne digne,
But in his techyng discreet and benynge.[26]

I was there to appreciate, to empathise and to understand. So, I bought a street map and borrowed a copy of the current electoral roll revealing which of the couples in prospect had yet to get married.

I need not, in the event, have been concerned. Visiting turned out to be easier than I thought. Most people were pleased to see me, though there was one unanticipated distraction. An advert featuring a parson was currently on ITV, advocating the virtues of Co-op tea. No sooner had the ersatz cleric arrived on the screen than he was confronted with a pot of tea, and so therefore was I. It had become the done thing, though not all the tealeaves, I imagined, were procured at the Co-op. The consequences were predictable, involving frequent and repeated visits to the loo. It was edifying, nevertheless. The college was mistaken, as was ITV. Most of the parishioners were hospitable, though they were somewhat surprised and taken aback. Parochial visiting from the clergy had not been done for many years.

On 4th September Ann was expected back in Yorkshire

26 From 'The Prologue', *The Canterbury Tales*, l, 514–18, translated by Gerald J. Davis: 'He was a shepherd and not a mercenary. And though he was holy, and virtuous, he was to sinful men nor scornful and his speech was not disdainful nor haughty, and in his teaching he was discrete and benign.'

for the beginning of term. So I arranged to meet her in Liverpool on the Tuesday before. She was there when I came down the gangway from the Mersey Ferry, her hair black as ravens, an unqualified vision of perfection in a short tweed coat and a pale lilac skirt. She never ceased to amaze me. We were only apart for a few weeks, but each renewed acquaintance was as if it were the first. Was not this the woman I had repeatedly missed lectures for? I thought of Puck's capricious potion in *A Midsummer Night's Dream*. But the mere hint of her was enough. Not for a moment was the enchantment between us undone. She was somehow less touchable and could afford a more extravagant lipstick. There was nothing more to it than that.

We talked to each other intensely and at length. Then we went into the department store, George Henry Lee's, where we bought an ultra-modern Danish chair, state of the art in metal and teak, the ultimate in minimalism with long metal spikes for legs and slim, pale, yellow cushions for the seat and the back. I couldn't afford it, but we loved it, the very first piece of furniture we could call our own.

'If we were to get married,' Ann said, 'you must bear one thought in mind. I'm a committed career woman. I don't expect ever to have children.'

I only half believed her, though she had said it many times before.

CHAPTER 11

The funeral

The chair was delivered to my flat the following week. Ginny thought it funny. The ubiquitous Fred decided he would sit nowhere else.

But the affairs of the parish took precedence in the weeks that followed. I was making progress. I was allowed to preach at St Mary's, though I was expected to submit my sermon to the vicar beforehand. Again, I did not mention it, but I persisted in my parochial visiting. Having started, there seemed no reason to stop.

One old lady was apocalyptic. She talked of nothing but the end of the world.

'It will be like the atom bomb,' she said. 'But it will not be from the Russians.'

By another I was propositioned. She was small, dumpy and unappetising.

'Why don't you come upstairs to the bedroom with me?' she said 'You have nothing to worry about. I have a Dutch cap.'[27]

She wanted me to visit her sister-in-law who would appreciate the same thing. As in *The News of the World*, I made my excuses and left.

27 A cervical contraceptive device which is not 100% effective.

There was also a more significant problem. I approached the project systematically, passing from one house to the next, beginning each morning in the Glanalyn estate on the edge of town. I was fulfilling my vocation, but the faithful were up in arms.

'Have you given up being our curate?' they said. 'You missed the Mothers' Union Coffee Morning. Where on earth have you been?'

Nor, I discovered, did the 'indifference' principle invariably apply. One day I was ushered in to meet Sir Bernard Eldon Franklin who presented me with a glass of sherry. A balding, moustached, affable man in a plain blue suit, he was managing director of a well-known banana importing company. His secretary came in soon after.

'Jamaica is on the phone, sir.'

He waved her away.

'Tell them to ring back. I'm talking to the curate.'

It left me with delusions of grandeur. But my housing estate visits were also beginning to have effect. It took an hour and a half whenever I went out to the shops. They had yet to attend the services, but the people I had visited approached me on the street, regaling me with the babies that were born, the geriatrics that were unwell, the multitudinous successes and hindrances of their lives. I was getting into the weft and weave of society, which made it abundantly clear. No wonder parochial visiting had been abandoned. There were far too many of them and a great deal too few of me. Chaucer's *povre persoun* was a dream. He could never have existed in the real world. But, there was, it transpired, more than visiting to the workings of a parochial ministry.

'It's time you took a funeral,' the vicar said. 'You've seen how it is done. Now you must conduct one for yourself.' He consulted his *Parson's Pocket Book*. 'There's one arranged for later this week. I've been to see the family. There's no point in you doing so as well.'

I was not sure about that, but I took him at his word. A widow called Emily Wyncome had died. The undertakers were William Arnold and Sons. The service was to take place on Thursday, 25th September, at eleven. The coffin was to be brought into St Mary's at six the evening before.

'After you have received the cortege,' he said, 'I expect you to lock up the church. We can't have people wandering about.' Then he added, as if by way of an afterthought, 'The undertaker will be issuing a cheque. Make sure it's payable to me.'

So that was it. Never before had it been made clear . . . I was to be the officiating minister, but I was not to receive the fee.

There was nothing untoward about it on the Wednesday evening as they arrived. I was introduced to Mrs Wyncome's daughters, Amelia, Charlotte and Winifred, mature blonde women in their late twenties or early thirties, evidently unmarried. They were suitably subdued as the bearers brought the coffin up the steps and into the church. I read out the sentences from *The Book of Common Prayer*. It was done decorously, without haste, preparatory to the obsequies the following day. Afterwards, Amelia came to speak to me in the vestry.

'We want to linger a little while longer,' she said.

I was not unsympathetic, but I there were several other things I had to do.

'I'm sorry, I can't wait around for long,' I said.

I was then accosted by all three.

'We want to reopen the coffin,' Charlotte said. 'We want to see the face of our lovely dear mother one more time. You cannot refuse us that.'

It seemed ridiculous. It must have remained open in the undertaker's chapel of rest. What would the vicar have done under the circumstances? I couldn't imagine him allowing it. But he was not there to consult. There was nothing else for it.

'I cannot agree to that,' I replied. 'It would be quite inappropriate. The remains of your deceased mother are now in the care of the church.'

With that all hell was let loose. They were going to write to the bishop. They were going to have me struck off. Excommunication was too good for me. I did all I could to quell the turmoil.

'I'm sorry,' I said. 'You must take it up with vicar. I am only the curate. I have my instructions. I am now required to lock up.'

It took some time. But finally, reluctantly, they went.

I was anticipating difficulties the following day, but there were none at the church where we followed convention with the funeral service, interspersed with 'The Lord's my shepherd' and 'Abide with me'. It was threatening rain as we emerged. I climbed into the passenger seat of the hearse. A gentle shower developed as we passed down the High Street. The pace was funereal, allowing Mr Arnold to come into his own. Wearing a topper and jet-black cape, reminiscent of the advert for Sandeman port, Mr Arnold halted our progress to have a quiet word with each bystander who did not doff his hat when we passed.

The rain was tippling down when we arrived at the cemetery, making it somewhat in the nature of a burial at sea. That was not my only predicament. Winifred was overcome with grief, caterwauling to high heaven. Mr Arnold conducted her away. Then Charlotte went into a swoon and was carried off by the men. Equally stricken, Amelia also disappeared. But no sooner had one sister gone than another came tottering back.

My surplice was soaked. There was nothing else for it. I ploughed my way through the solemn words of the committal: 'In sure and certain hope of the resurrection to eternal life . . .' Thus, despite all the turmoil, the deceased Mrs Wyncome was laid peacefully to rest. I wanted to speak to the sisters afterwards, but they were whisked away in a car by the undertakers. Refreshments were laid on at a nearby pub. I was not invited. So I returned to the flat to get changed.

'How did you get on?' the vicar asked when I gave him the cheque.

'It was a bit of a do,' I said.

He nodded. 'I thought it might be.'

So that was it. He had anticipated it all along. What did Neville Bithell say? 'He expects his curates to be prepared for any eventuality.' It left me puzzled, nevertheless. I had expected to comfort the bereaved. It had not been possible.

'Those girls led their mother a dog's life while she was alive,' somebody said.

CHAPTER 12

Among the sundry and manifold changes of the world . . .

The following week there were problems at the flat. One of the doctors from the surgeries threw grit at my kitchen window and shouted up at me. His patients objected to my loud playing of the Bechstein. Then there were conflicts at the Parochial Church Council. There had been much talk about it for months. St Mary's may have been the epitome of mediaeval art, but the churchyard was a scrapheap of broken and decaying gravestones. The vicar wanted them removed. There were loud and strong objections from the brigadier. Then, on the following Saturday, I was confronted with a dilemma at the church of St James. That they were pleased to see me made it more difficult. The New Brightonites were in the midst of a sea of mops, buckets, brushes, tins of polish, vacuum cleaners and feather dusters, voluntarily out to give their church a good clean. So how could I apportion blame when I was met with such evident goodwill? I spoke out loudly and firmly.

'Why are all the lightbulbs in this church stolen from Courtaulds?' I asked.

If I had hoped for an answer, I got none. The women looked tentative.

'You had better ask Fred about it,' somebody said. In conjunction with Frank, Fred was the people's warden, an ungainly, well-intentioned man who worked for a local builder. Nor was he inclined to get involved.

'You had better ask John about it,' was all he would say . . . which brought me to John William Faulkner, the organist, a white-haired, thick set man who, it transpired, was a shop steward at the Courtaulds Castle Works in Flint.

'It's not at all surprising,' he said. 'The management doesn't show the workers the slightest respect,[28] which is why every moveable object in the factory is marked, "Stolen from Courtaulds". It's quite stupid. If you invite people to steal, they will do exactly that. Go around this village, you will find stuff of all kinds lifted from the factory, tools, fittings, crockery, cutlery, even pots of jam. You name it. It's nicked from Courtaulds.'

It seemed outrageous.

'But people are responsible for their actions,' I said. 'They cannot blame them on the antics of the management.' A more immediate point struck me. 'Nor can we harbour stolen

28 cf *The British Medical Journal*, 1968. Courtaulds' use of carbon disulfide for the manufacture of viscose rayon exposed their work force to heart attacks, strokes and mental illness.

property in the church. Is there some way I can return it?'

This seemed to amuse him.

'I wouldn't even try. You'll get yourself prosecuted.'

'You did the only thing possible,' the vicar said when I told him about it. 'Not on any account should we enter into litigation with Courtaulds. Their lawyers would make hay of us . . . though I agree, their policy leaves much to be desired.'

He said no more about it than that. I was not surprised. It had become apparent. He and the New Brightonites did not get on. It was quite unreasonable on his part. I don't think he objected to games of chance, but tombola he positively excoriated, thinking it pernicious and a total waste of time. So he would not allow them to hold bingo sessions in their hall in aid of church funds. Feelings ran high. There was nothing more to it than that. Yet the New Brightonites would not let it go. Nor did they have the slightest respect for his authority. So they supplied the prizes and collected the dividends from the bingo in the neighbouring parish of Northup. But even that did not satisfy them.

'You come and take our services,' said old Mrs Johnson who lived on the edge of the village, 'and keep that vicar away from our church.' She smiled at me beatifically. 'You remind me of the lovely Evan David who used to be our curate years ago. It was he who began the eggs and flowers.'

It explained a lot. The Eggs and Flowers were among the least of his crimes. The Reverend Canon Evan David Jenkins, MA, BD, known for his perversity and contempt for punctuation, was vicar of St Mary's, Bangor, while I was at the university. We used to attend his services for the pleasure of it, savouring particularly his high speed, high octane 'throughjesuschristourlordamenourfather'. Nor was that his only delinquency. On one occasion, generating the same screechy ebullience, he asked us whether we would prefer five wise virgins in the light or five foolish virgins in the dark. None of us had the slightest reservations about that. The New Brightonites might have thought highly of him, but the Reverend Canon's oddities put me in my place, reminding me there were no great merits to my popularity.

CHAPTER 13

. . . Where true joys are to be found

In mid-September, I began to prepare for the exam prior to my ordination to the priesthood the following May. Among the set books was *St John's Gospel: A Commentary* by RH Lightfoot,[29] where the biblical narrative was treated like an innovative novel where each episode encapsulates the features of the drama as a whole. Christ's incarnation, his mission and his victory in the face of defeat were seen as recurrent leitmotifs within the piece. I found Lightfoot's analysis extraordinary, placing the Gospel at odds with every other literary work of the period. St John's Gospel is different in style from the synoptic[30] Gospels of Matthew, Mark and Luke, exhibiting affinities instead with the Johannine[31] writings of the New Testament. Lightfoot mentions such matters but

29 Oxford, 1956

30 Giving an account of events from the same perspective

31 the Gospel according to St John, the Epistles general of John 1,11 and 111, and the Book of the Revelation of St John the Divine

confines his observations to 'a religious and theological exposition of the text'.

But there was one peculiar advantage to the work. I found it an incomparable source of sermon making, a point I was to exploit when, in the vicar's absence, it was left to me to take Evensong at St Mary's for the very first time. He and his wife Linda were quite excited. Evidently, it was something of an occasion. They were invited to an anniversary dinner and were likely to stay on afterwards. He did not enquire about my sermon. I was left to make of it what I could. I found it quite stimulating as I climbed into the oaken vastness of the pulpit. I used the episode where Jesus, while making his way through the Samaritan hill country, encounters a woman at Jacob's well. I began by painting the scene, the deep rock-hewn well excavated in mountainous countryside used by itinerant shepherds for the watering of their flocks, believed from time immemorial to be quarried by the patriarch Jacob. The water lay some distance below, requiring the use of a bucket and a rope, which explained why Jesus began by asking the woman for a drink of water out of the well. She was surprised. It was unusual for a Jew to speak to a Samaritan. But he had more momentous matters in mind.

> *If thou knewest the gift of God, and who it is that saith to thee, Give me to drink; thou wouldest have asked of him, and he would have given thee living water.*[32]

32 John 4, 10

It was a pivotal moment. As Lightfoot points out, figurative references to water appeared throughout the early chapters of St John's Gospel. The Baptist baptised with water at Bethabara beyond Jordan. Water became wine at the wedding in Cana of Galilee. At Ænon near Salim, the Baptist and Jesus baptised in a place where 'there was much water'. The woman was no angel, having had five husbands while the man she lived with was not her husband, but she was intelligent and receptive. Their conversation culminates in Jesus' transformational promise of 'a well of water, springing up into everlasting life'. I made a great deal of the metaphor in the course of my sermon. Afterwards, people congratulated me on my first lone Evensong in the parish church.

But I was reprimanded by Miss Georgina Prince.

'I was quite put out,' she said. 'You could have chosen something less provocative. You went on about it for far too long. You have simply no idea. I was utterly parched, longing throughout your discourse for a glass of water.'

The following day I met an old man on the High Street.

'I'm told I must congratulate you,' he said. 'They say you preached very well, though it wasn't entirely proper. The woman in your sermon was a tart.' He studied me solemnly. 'But the old dears have a point. In a large public building like that you should have a loo.'

He was right. I heard about it afterwards. The redoubtable Mrs Joan Wellesley-Davies did not mention it. It was said she was dying for a pee.

But the grain of an idea was rooted in my mind. It was irresistible, the instinct of the moment. The vicar and his wife had not returned. On the following Wednesday I bought a ring from one of the market traders. I thought it quite beautiful, the bezel in a curved knot encrusted with deep blue sapphires and a cluster of tiny diamonds. I had no idea whether I had received value for money. Nor did I care. It was anarchical, the point of no return when I went AWOL after I had said Mattins the following day, taking a train that brought me through Chester to Crewe. My thoughts were racing. The engine never seemed to pick up steam. It was excruciatingly slow. I was famished. There was no dining car. Hours later, by way of the Dorman-Long Steelworks in Redcar, I finally arrived in Saltburn-by-the-Sea. Ann was astonished. She advised me to take a room at The Spa Hotel.

I poured her a glass of wine when she joined me later for a meal. A band struck up in the ballroom of the hotel. There was nothing else for it. It was probably a strange sight as I swept her onto the floor. Appraising my dog collar, people gave me sideways looks. I didn't care. She was in my arms, ravishing in a white chiffon dress. We went dancing every Saturday night while we were at the university. It was as though we had never stopped. Bopping had become all the rage. But we danced to an old tune, Irving Berlin's 'Change Partners' . . . though we would not have exchanged each other for the world. There was delight in her face. I loved her lips, her embrace, the cadences, the lilt of the music, the cursive treatment of the words. We returned to our table. I produced the ring in its box.

'Can I give you this?'

There were tears and laughter in her eyes.

'You should go down on one knee.' Then she hesitated. 'You know it's a dress ring? It's not an engagement ring.'

'I don't care what it is. I love it . . . and I love you. Will you marry me?'

Her response was pure romance. She handed me back the ring.

'I'm stupid even to think of it,' she said as I put it on the third finger of her left hand.

'We'll be married in the Spring,' I promised, 'on the Saturday after Easter.'

CHAPTER 14

Thereafter

The return journey involved the same unrelenting grind in reverse. But I was euphoric. Ann and I were engaged. I arrived back in the parish at about four in the afternoon. Mr Jason had noticed my absence. It was not surprising. He lived in a tall, dilapidated house alongside the steps leading up to the church. Did it matter? I thought not. He had an obstreperous wife and other problems. I was faced with a dilemma, nevertheless. Mattins had not been said on the morning I was away. Nor could I bring myself to falsify an entry in the parish register. But . . . there was also something else. I had deserted my post, a dereliction of duty. I tried to reassure myself. No appreciable harm had been done. It was wrong for all that. Nor could I know what the vicar might say. He and Lynda were back soon after six. I saw their ramshackle Standard Vanguard as it swept up the driveway towards the vicarage. And then? The fifteenth Sunday after Trinity was uneventful.

But it was a game of cat and mouse. There was a calculating look in the vicar's eye when we met for our staff meeting the following day.

'I understand you were away from the parish on Thursday night, Mr Hughes. Such things do not go unnoticed. People are talking about it in the town. I know you caught a train. Where did you go and why?'

There seemed no point in obfuscating.

'Ann and I have decided to get married on 4th April next year, the Saturday after Easter.'

He was surprised.

'I see. It was that important . . . a proposal of marriage no less. You went all the way up to Yorkshire to do that?' There was a protracted silence as he considered it. 'There was no need to make off. You could easily have discussed it with me.'

'But Ann might have said no.'

He shook his head.

'What a thing it is to be young.' He reached for his *Parson's Pocketbook*. 'Will the ceremony take place in Bootle? It is customary for weddings to be solemnised in the bride's parish church.'

I knew nothing of her local parish. Nor, I suspected, did Ann.

He took a seat at his paper strewn desk and looked up at me.

'You know you will need the bishop's permission.' Then, suddenly, he smiled. 'I won't raise any objections. So neither, I suspect, will he.'

'Why do I need the bishop's permission?'

'You must surely have anticipated it. You're a deacon in the probationary year of your ministry. There are implications to such things. Your proposed wife should be a dedicated member of the church.' He gave it a moment's thought. 'I suggest you write to the bishop. Make certain you address the letter correctly. He is "The Right Reverend Father in God". You are his most "humble and obedient servant".'

Of one thing I was certain as I returned to the flat. I was not prepared to discuss Ann's disbeliefs. They were nobody's problem but mine. Nor was that my only obstacle. I don't think there was a woman on earth that could have met with my mother's approval. She had long made her objections known to Ann's décolletage. I remembered their first encounter while we were at the university.

'If you will insist on taking up with some girl, try to find someone more suitable.'

There was one curious aspect to it. The atmosphere was frigid when Ann came to stay at the vicarage. But she was more agitated by the bedroom where a rope in the form of a noose was hanging over her bed.

'Don't be ridiculous,' I said. 'It is not unusual in a period building like this. You pulled the rope to summon a maid, in the days when the clergy could afford to employ domestic staff.'

'But why is it a noose?'

'I've no idea. The ropes are looped like that in all the bedrooms, probably knotted by somebody with a morbid sense of humour.'

It was Ann's one and only visit to the vicarage. She stayed only a few days. Unsurprisingly, she loved the church.

I gave my mother some thought as I boarded the bus that took me to the village. She may have been undemonstrative, but she could be something of a character when she had the bit between her teeth. It was amazing how she managed the bleak cold vicarage of my childhood during the war, at Rhosygwalia near Bala where my father was vicar. There was no mains electricity. We survived on paraffin lamps. Water had to be pumped up by hand out of the river. The work was unrelenting. Washing on a Monday used to take most of the day. A fire was lit under the stone boiler in a corner of the wash-kitchen. Dollies were used to pummel the clothes. If the weather was wet, shirts, towels, dresses, knickers and long johns were hung around the house. My mother was helped by Nellie Thomas, a little wizened old woman that came up from the village. She gave us our first inkling of the war . . . embroiling the heroic, cigar-smoking Mr Turtle and the miscreant Harry Hitler that needed a good kick up the pants.

My mother was mixing a cake when I arrived.

'Ann and I are engaged,' I said.

Had she been expecting it? She stared at me blankly and pursed her lips. There was always something about her. She had once been a flapper, given to bobbed hair, cloche hats and Charlestons. She retained something of the style.

'You'd better go and tell your father.'

I had expected recriminations. She said no more about it than that. He was in the yard, a crouching, crumbling figure, feeding the hens.

'Ann and I are going to be married,' I said, 'on the Saturday after Easter next year.'

There was a bleak look in his eye.

'Where will this marriage take place?'

'I don't know. It has yet to be decided.'

He shook his head. Again, nothing was said. It took me some moments to appreciate it. It was the parting of the waves. Never was there a father less unlikely to interfere in his son's affairs. Yet he said nothing. It was depressing, heart rending. He may not have liked it, but it was abundantly clear: no longer was I his responsibility.

My mother returned to her baking after lunch while we sat together in my father's study. It was difficult to know what to talk about.

'You still need to raise more money,' I said, 'and this is a very small community.'

The change of topic seemed to ease him. He nodded.

'Cilcain used to be much more extensive. Several other parishes were carved out of it in the nineteenth century.'

That I had not known. An idea struck me.

'Think about the parishioners that were taken out. They may be on different electoral rolls, but the names of their forebears remain in your parish records.' It seemed quite exciting. 'Do you have any old registers? Perhaps you could hold an exhibition, rouse public interest, make a fuss about it in the press. It might help with the fundraising.'

He pondered this for a moment then scrabbled around in a box on the mantelpiece to find a key. A sepia picture of the village street in 1923 was hung over a safe in the corner, sunk into the wall. I had forgotten it was there. Never had I seen it opened.

'Wilkinson, my predecessor, was a stupid man,' he said. 'This should not be in the vicarage. It ought to be in the parish church where it belongs.'

He thrust the key into the lock and swung open the door. Undoubtedly, he was right. They should not have been in the vicarage. It was packed with archives. He waved a hand.

'The current registers are in the church safe. These have come down to us from the past.' He picked out a substantial leather-bound tome. 'This is the original parish register.'

We stood together at his desk to ponder the contents. Apart from anything else, it was a history of handwriting. The entries from the reign of Elizabeth I were the most difficult to make out.

'They're in Secretary Hand,' my father explained. 'Shakespeare composed his plays in secretary. But when he wrote to Ann Hathaway, he went into italic. Italic, the Italian style, was considered a lady's hand.'

I was surprised.

'I thought Ann Hathaway was illiterate.'

He shrugged his shoulders and gave me a grin. The registers were mostly in English, but they went into Latin for a period early in the eighteenth century, by which time the style was italic copperplate.

Unlike the present where they were recorded separately, the baptisms, marriages and funerals occupied different sections within the same book. Nor were the entries formally laid out, their treatment quite perfunctory. But there were a great many other items to engage our attention.

'At one time the parish employed a full-time mole catcher,' I said. 'A lot seems to have been spent on exterminating vermin, though it's difficult to gauge how much it would cost in modern money. In 1732, John Williams was paid four shillings and four pence for the of killing four foxes and two fischets. I wonder what was meant by a fischet.'

'It was probably a fox cub,' my father replied. He flipped over the pages. 'For practically the same price in 1711, they paid four shillings and six pence for rushes to be strewed on the floor of the church. That could be quite hazardous.'

He turned to the opening page.

'This register begins in 1576, but we have it on record that at daybreak on Christmas Day 1532, the north aisle was burnt down following a plygain.[33] There can be little doubt about it. The rushes must have spread the fire.'

We continued to study the register.

'We're a long way from the south coast of England,' I said. 'Yet there's a note in 1588 about the coming of the Spanish Armada.'

He nodded.

'The whole country,' he replied, 'was in turmoil. A beacon

33 A Welsh celebration of the Nativity which, traditionally, took place at daybreak on Christmas Day. The carols are unaccompanied, unique, passed down from one generation to the next. Plygains now take place in the evening sometime during the Christmas season.

was set up on the top of Moel Famau.'[34]

A smile appeared on his face.

'Your vicar is forever talking about the antiquity of Mold Parish Church. He should compare it to ours. Cilcain's circular churchyard places its origins in pre-Christian times.'

I had heard that before, shades of prehistoric dolmens and Stonehenge, though it was difficult to imagine what that implied.

'Apart from the parish records,' my father said, 'there are marks on the external wall of the north aisle where, at one time, people played some kind of game, though we can have no idea of the rules.'

I gave it some thought as I came away. There was one problem. It was difficult to understand. The mediaeval roof over the south aisle could be dated to around 1470. So how, some fifty years later, had the angels and hammerbeams survived the incineration of the north aisle? It must have been there if the roof was locally built. I discussed it that evening with Ann over the phone.

'I know you don't think so,' she said, 'but perhaps it really was brought from that abbey near Holywell.'

I could not but disagree.

'The records prove it,' I said. 'The fire in the north aisle took place on Christmas Day 1532. But Basingwerk Abbey was not dissolved until 1536. Nor could such a structure have been shifted overnight.' There was one further point

34 the highest peak of the Clwydian Range, overlooking the village

to it. 'I think I know the origins of the tale. An Anglesey poet called Robin Ddu[35] prophesied that the refectory roof at Basingwerk would go to a church "below Moel Famau".[36] But he wrote that some eighty years earlier. It was a flight of fancy. The monasteries were not under threat.'

'I love those quirky angels,' she chuckled. 'One of them has a distinct squint.'

35 fl c 1450

36 *'o dan Moel Famau'*

CHAPTER 15

Like an ever-rolling stream . . .

The weeks thereafter passed quickly, the Harvest Festivals, Advent, Christmas. The harvest hymns and the carols epitomised the moment, marking the seasons with 'Come ye thankful people come' and 'tidings of comfort and joy', though by their sheer repetition I had had enough of them by the time their moment was past. Of the festivals I found Christmas the most inspirational. There was so prodigious a richness to it, St Mary's incandescent in holly and ribbonry, the great seasonal pine cascading its approbation in baubles and lights. But there was also an irony to it . . . amid the great display of affluence was the crib and the glowing virgin marking the poverty of his birth. Nor could I forget its transience, the Disneyesque reindeers and Santas about to be jettisoned with the cards and minced pies.

Finally, at St Mary's at the Midnight Mass, I read the appointed text from the Epistle to the Hebrews,[37] a letter not addressed to any known recipients:

37 Hebrews is a homiletic commentary on Psalm 110. Somebody added Chapter 13 to accommodate the New Testament pattern of Epistles and Gospels.

> *God who at sundry times and in divers manners spake in time past unto the fathers by the prophets, hath in these last days spoken unto us by his Son, whom he hath appointed heir of all things, by whom also he made the worlds . . .*

How could I argue with that?

'Wherefore,' adds the author of Hebrews, reinforcing it, 'we are also compassed about with so great a cloud of witnesses . . .'

It was the principle of my education, forever learning from those that knew what I had yet to understand. Patently, it was not enough. All I could do was believe. There was no rationality to it any more than there was a rationality to my love for Ann. For 'by love may he be gotten and holden, but by thought never,' writes the anonymous author of *The Cloud of Unknowing*. I could not yet aspire to deeper mysteries, the dark night quest of St John of the Cross:

> *Upon an obscure night,*
> *Fevered with love's anxiety,*
> *Oh happy, hapless plight!*
> *I went, none seeing me,*
> *Forth from my house*
> *Where all things quiet be.*[38]

I must remain content with what I had.

38 tr John Martlew

The vicar preached a long, platitudinous sermon. When the Midnight Mass was over, I was invited to the vicarage for a miniscule glass of sherry and a minced pie. I finally got to bed at about two thirty, and, at six, I joined the postal staff at the sorting office for carols before they set out to deliver the last of the Christmas mail. I was happy.

CHAPTER 16

Onwards as to war . . .

I spent the week after Christmas with Ann's family at her home in Bootle. She was no less enchanting than ever. But it was not particularly amorous. If my mother had her objections to her, no less did her mother and sisters have their reservations about me. That we were officially engaged made little difference. Nor did they seem much to like the Welsh.

On my return I was expected to take part in the watchnight service at St Mary's, obliging me to refuse invitations to the various New Year's Eve parties that were taking place around the town. It left me feeling abandoned and isolated, languishing alone in the flat with a proverbial 'good book', in the event an interesting reassessment of Jesus' parables . . . small compensation when the rest of the world was out having a ball. The vicar took the service and I read the prayers to usher in 1959.

I caught up with Peter and Nancy Croft on the way out. I knew him a little, a dour, taciturn man who was manager of Boots on the High Street. She was markedly his antithesis, a lively demonstrative woman, amply powdered and perfumed, dressed in an opulent fur coat and absurdly diminutive fur hat.

'You, poor darling,' she said, tucking my hand proprietorially under her arm. 'We left a party to come to the service.

But you've not even had a drink. Come back to our place. There will be only the three of us, but we won't give up until we're well and truly rat-arsed.'

So, I did. I have not the slightest idea what time I got to bed. Nor do I recall much of what happened, though I remember telling them about the Christmas card I received from Father Tom.

'He wished me a happy circumcision,' I said, which, after I had explained it,[39] they thought was very funny.

Somehow, I got up in time for Morning Prayer. The vicar was bleary-eyed.

The Second Sunday after Christmas was sparsely attended, but the vicar was in a lively mood when we met at the vicarage the following day.

'It is a time for new beginnings, Mr Hughes,' he said. 'You must therefore make the necessary arrangements for the setting up of a youth club. It should be a sheer joy. I recall with pleasure the days when I was an assistant curate before the war, during which time I had the care of a delightful fellowship of young people. You could find no more convivial an assembly of the junior church.'

I thought it an excellent idea, my first practical contribution to parish life, though what he said about his youth club would not do at all. It was far too benign, too objectionably middle class. We lived in more pragmatic times. Hitler had seen to that. There was an officially sponsored

39 1st January is the 'Feast of the Circumcision'.

youth organisation called 'Cymru'r Groes', though in so anglicised a part of Wales it seemed inappropriate. I must therefore work it out for myself.

I advertised the proposed youth club in the days that followed with notices in the shops and, on the following Sunday, with announcements at the services. Rosie came to see me at the flat. My instinct was to put her off. There was no way she could usurp Ann, but I felt a responsibility for her. There was no denying it, though. Her aspirations were shared by half the young women in the town. They continued to crowd the services and I was forever meeting their eyes in the street. It was ironic. Mr Bithell was pleased with the improvement in the collections.

'This is my friend Vicky,' Rosie said. 'We want to help you make a start.'

In a fussy, unshapely red frock, Vicky was plump, tongue-tied and shy. Nor was there anything distinctive about Rosie ... small-framed and dark haired with a stubby freckled nose, she was dressed in a little black pinafore dress. She was aged around eighteen or nineteen, though she looked younger. Her mother had summed her up well: a hostage as ever to love's young dream.

Suspending my reservations, we went down to the church hall on King Street where the club was to meet. I already knew something of it as a determinedly gloomy building originating as a Gothic Revival church converted for use as a hall. Its recycling, I was told, together with the concomitant fundraising, was the work of enthusiastic volunteers. But there was no disguising its origins, consecrated as a place of worship some ninety years earlier to serve the indigenous Welsh. That I found outrageous. If the great scintillating church of St Mary's was endowed by Lady Margaret Beaufort to mark her son's accession to the English throne, by what principle was it thought proper that his compatriots should be reduced to ecclesiastical Victoriana?

The inference could not have been more emphatic. The Welsh may have played their part at Bosworth, but other considerations had taken precedence from the start, pointing the way to an established English national church, which explained why the majority of the Welsh adopted the chapel. What did they say about the churchgoers? 'You're a Tory. You pray for the Queen'.[40] But that too had its ramifications. The renowned nineteenth century novelist Daniel Owen was born and brought up in Mold. He probed, with a certainty of touch, life under an austere Welsh-speaking Calvinistic Methodism, the measure against which everything they did was judged. There was nevertheless an integrity and warmth to his characters, projecting a profound sense of community and fellowship:

'Rhys,' my mother said, looking at me chasteningly, 'I've never before caught you telling a lie. Do you want to break your mother's heart?'[41]

40 *'Tori wyt ti, yn gweddio am y frenhinness.'*

41 *'Rhys,' ebe fy mam, gan edrych yn geryddgar arnaf, 'daru mi rioed o'r blaen dy ddal di yn dweyd anwiredd. Ai isio tori calon dy fam yr wyt ti?'* Hunangofiant Rhys Lewis, 1885, tr Stephen Owen, 2015.

I was moved at the thought of it. Yet by the late 1950s, not only were the chapels in decline, but, perhaps because of the town's proximity to the English border, it was a rarity to hear Welsh spoken in the street.

'It's not what you'd call modern,' Rosie said, bringing me back to the present.

The hall would suit our purposes, nevertheless. The club, we decided should meet on Friday evenings at seven.

CHAPTER 17

The unruly wills and affections . . .

On Monday 12th January at ten-thirty in the morning, supplanting our weekly staff meeting at the vicarage, I attended the Assize Service[42] at St Mary's. It was important. The bishop was present. As it was a notable ceremonial occasion, the vicar and I wore surplice, stole and academic hood, while the bishop, crozier in hand, was in a chimere,[43] rochet[44] and tippet,[45] decorative cope and mitre. We looked magnificent. Mr Jason issued us printed copies of the order of service. The organist launched into Bach's 'Toccata and Fugue in D minor' as we followed the choristers in solemn procession to take our places in the stalls. The vicar conducted the bishop to his episcopal throne in the sanctuary.

42 The Assize Courts were abolished with *The Courts Act* 1971, to be replaced by a single, permanent Crown Court.

43 a loose sleeveless robe

44 a white surplice-like robe

45 a ceremonial scarf

To the mellifluous tones of S.S. Wesley's 'Lead me, Lord, in thy righteousness', the Judge of the Assize, the Honourable Sir Percy Gerald Moncrieff, CBE, was led by the verger to take his seat in the front pew of the nave. He was attended by the High Sheriff, John Jeremiah Moss, Esq, Roger's successor, accompanied by his chaplain, the Reverend James Morgan Evans, BA. The only person I recognised among the entourage was Henry Philip Gold, a droopy local solicitor who was designated Under Sheriff. (My mother called him a twit.) There was an awesome solemnity to it, choreographed like the setting out of pieces on a chess board.

We proceeded to a truncated version of Morning Prayer. The vicar delivered the opening sentence: 'Owe no man anything, but to love one another: for love is the fulfilling of the law.'[46] I intoned the responses. The choristers sang the psalm, 'My song shall be of mercy and judgement.'[47] The bishop came down to the read the lesson, 'Let every soul be subject to the higher powers . . .',[48] delivered in his funny little voice, which was perhaps why, in the aftermath, I had my reservations about the whole procedure. The scriptures epitomised judicious perfection. It was not consistent with the real world. Later that day, the judge would pass summary judgement on the assortment of petty criminals

46 Romans 13, 8

47 Psalms 101, 1

48 Romans, 13, 1

that were brought before him.

But the role of the parson is insular, hived away from the rest of humanity by his vocation and dog collar. It explained the vicar's enthusiasm for chapter meetings where the clergy of the deanery met monthly for communal study and fellowship. These were usually held in one or other of the vicarages, but the venue the following Wednesday, the first of the year, was St Deiniol's Residential Library, Hawarden, the sprawling neo-Gothic pile where I spent my pre-ordination retreat. Built in the aftermath of his death, the brainchild of William Ewart Gladstone,[49] the purpose was to provide visiting scholars with bed and board entrée to his extensive collection of books, mostly theology. I could not bring myself to like the place. The library and the public rooms remained splendid, but the domestic quarters were bleak, labyrinthine and cold. I thought it oppressive. Gothic Revival was never my proclivity, evocative of an overblown hubris and a permanently accumulating stock exchange. It was as though the kingdom of heaven was arrogated into their real estates:

Solid joys and lasting treasure
None but Zion's people know.[50]

The chapters of the clergy on the other hand, a taxonomy

49 intermittently prime minister 1868–94

50 John Newton, 1779, A&M 257

we held in common with the Hell's Angels, were altogether more modest affairs, fostering a sense of communal fellowship among us while encouraging our interest in recently published theology. The morning of the meeting was notable for a sharp frost, sending us huddling around the amply stoked-up coal fires at each extremity of the library's extensive, double fireplaced lounge, redolent of a myriad ancient jokes where Satan couldn't see the fire for parsons. Finally, we were enticed to take our seats by the Rural Dean, the Reverend Richard Sinnet Wilson, Vicar of Rhydymwyn, who opened the proceedings with prayer, a white-haired priest with an amply padded stomach and a voice reminiscent of Larry the Lamb.

'The meeting next month, brethren,' he said, 'falls on February 11th which is Ash Wednesday. I know you will be holding services in your own parish churches, but there is no reason why we should not also meet as a chapter. I propose therefore we foregather at eleven at St Deiniol's Church, Hawarden, where we can, as stipulated in the prayerbook, make it our business to read "The Commination".'

It came as a surprise. With the exception of Stainer's setting of 'The Churching of Women', I had no more than glanced at the occasional services of *The Book of Common Prayer*. I knew only that 'The Commination' anathematises, that is liturgically curses, all the wrongdoings of humanity. It was more appropriate, I thought, to an age of inquisitions than to the faith of the church in the modern world. No longer should it be seen as proper to eviscerate a man's body in order to save his soul.

The Very Reverend James Grimsdyke Enstone, Dean Emeritus of St Asaph, then introduced us to *The Parables of Jesus* by Joachim Jeremias, the book recently earmarked for study. Having dipped into my copy on New Year's Eve, I knew what to expect: a German scholar's reassessment of the parables, placing them within the context in which Jesus lived and showing how they were interpreted by the evangelists of the New Testament. I was reminded of the aftermath to my sermon about Jesus' encounter with the Samaritan woman. What I said was one thing. How I was understood was another. But when it came to his exposition of Jesus' parables, Jeremias was rather cleverer than that, demonstrating the way in which the process could be wound back so that their original meanings could be revisited.

The dean was emphatic. The synoptic Gospels are misleading when it came to the parable of the sower. The inference seemed obvious . . . Christians must be like the good seed that falls into good ground and flourishes accordingly.

'We should not be surprised,' the dean continued. 'They were writing later in the first century for the congregations of churches in such cities as Corinth, Ephesus or Rome. So they made their message clear. Christians must be like the good seed that falls into good land. The more assiduously they comply, the more profitable they are. The rule was simple. Christians must persevere, do their duty, pay their dues, do everything they could to further the life of the church.'

He smiled and nodded.

'It's mixed message, nevertheless. The faithful are compared to seeds. Yet where a seed falls is fortuitous, thrown anywhere and everywhere by the sower . . . which suggests they became Christians by chance. But the scriptures as we have them are flawed. You will notice the difference. Jesus was talking to the people of the Galilean countryside for whom such considerations meant nothing at all. There was no such thing as the church. They were not required to persevere. Also, as Jeremias points out, unlike farmers elsewhere it was their custom to sow the seed onto unploughed land. The stones, the thorns and the wayside were to be ploughed up afterwards . . . which makes a nonsense of the parable as it appears in the pages of the New Testament. The more difficult terrain was to be broken up with the passage of the plough. So let us envisage it. Jesus is standing in the prow of a boat some distance from the shore of the Sea of Galilee. Great crowds are standing at the lakeside waiting to hear his words.'

'Perhaps a seedsman is casting his seed on a nearby hillside. Jesus ribs the local farmers as he speaks: "Isn't that man an idiot? He paid good money for that grain. And what is he doing with it? He's throwing it away." You can imagine the country people laughing.'

The dean smiled.

'So, the meaning,' he continued, 'is plain. God grants his

gifts liberally to mankind just as a sower casts his seed willy nilly over the land. Jesus was talking about God's generosity, the profusion of riches he bestows on mankind. That is not to denigrate the evangelists. Both meanings were appropriate to the people for whom they were meant.'

'I prefer Jesus' version,' Ann said afterwards. 'It's the same old pie in the sky, but at least he wasn't after their money.'

CHAPTER 18

Thy way, not mine

That the youth club was a success there was no doubt. Rosie was at the heart of it, rounding them up so that already we had a membership of about fifty. She also rustled up a record player and piles of forty-fives, grinding out Elvis' 'Love me tender' irritatingly interspersed with Frankie Vaughan's 'The green door'. The members played cards, held quizzes and sometimes I invited guest speakers.

But again, I was confronted with fallible humanity. Many of them had brought packets of cigarettes. Having repeatedly failed to give up smoking, I knew of its tyranny. I was aware, too, that there were laws governing the use of tobacco among minors, though nobody, it seemed, took the slightest notice. I tried to treat the issue democratically . . . to no effect.

'My dad gives me a packet of fags a week,' Ivor said.

'My mum isn't particularly bothered,' said Winnie.

Smoking in the club became the norm. It was not ideal. It reflected the *status quo*. Underage smoking was regulated by law and proscribed by the schools, but you could retexture your clothes with teenage cigarette smoke at the Savoy Cinema on a Saturday night.

Another quandary arose soon after. The stage had been built over the Victorian chancel. There were thick red curtains to allow for the presentation of plays and concerts. But they were also put to further use, masking the assignations and canoodlings that took place among members of the club. Again, I made concessions to human nature. Nor did they greatly concern me until I received a letter from one of the parents.

> *My dear Mr Hughes,*
> *It was with some reluctance that I agreed to allow my fourteen-year-old daughter Cristabelle to enrol as a member of your youth club, thinking that on Friday evenings at least she would be under your careful personal supervision. You will appreciate my disappointment on discovering that that is by no means the case . . .*

It was signed Marianne Elspeth Holland. I knew Cristabelle was one of the amorous liaisons brigade. But it soon became clear: there was a great deal more to it than that. A headstrong, amply endowed blonde who smoked incessantly, she was all over an engagingly swarthy Italian called Ronaldo, aged seventeen. Her mother was adamant. They must be separated immediately. It was up to me to see to it. Could I not suspend Ronaldo's membership? There was one further aspect to it. The Hollands owned a house on suburban Bryn Coch Lane. Ronaldo lived on the Glanalyn council estate.

Since he was a Roman Catholic, I had already given Ronaldo's membership some thought. I had no objections to his allegiance to another church, but there was a question to be answered nevertheless. Had I, overtaking my responsibilities as curate, taken on the role of a social worker in charge of a youth club open to all? It was a matter of principle to which I didn't know the answer. Perhaps, in the interest of the public good, I should be prepared to fulfil both roles. But the problem of Cristabelle's amours was the more pressing.

Also, the weather had taken a turn for the worse. There was snow on the ground when I went to visit Mrs Holland the following Monday afternoon. My feet were freezing as I stood at her front door. There was more than a hint of her daughter about her: blonde, a figure running a little too fat, no less determined when it came to having her own way. But things had evidently moved on. She did not invite me in.

'I have nothing to say to you, Mr Hughes. You will not be surprised to hear that Cristabelle has resigned from your youth club. I will be bringing the matter up at the Parochial Church Council.'

It was quite upsetting. I needed to talk about it. I had always always been appreciative of Roger Parker, indicative perhaps of the respect that one profession might have for another. I was nevertheless conscious of the differences between us, the tangible practicalities of medicine as against the ethereal soul searchings of theology, the disparity too between his affluence and my poverty. On a day-to-day basis it made little difference. That evening we sat there as usual, absorbing the antics of the outrageous Fyfe Robinson and Alan Wicker's unabashed man about town. Afterwards, I told him about my encounter with Mrs Holland.

'As you will appreciate, I've not done anything wrong,' I said. 'It's not my fault that her daughter is something of a handful.'

'Parsons and doctors must expect such quandaries. People invariably think we're to blame,' he said sympathetically. He raised a crooked finger, requiring me to light him another cigarette. 'I was once called out to a vicarage in the country, miles from anywhere. I arrived at about two in the morning to find the vicar shouting at his wife with a Bible in one hand and a heavy school bell in the other.' He chuckled.

That I too found funny. For once I knew more about it than he did.

'Did he have a candle?'

His face confirmed it.

'It was not liturgically correct,' I said. 'It requires a bishop and twelve priests to excommunicate a heretic with bell, book and candle.'[51]

He looked surprised.

'Probably. I never did look into the protocol. I merely had him taken into the hospital for nervous disorders.'

'The loony bin in Denbigh?'

51 The bell drew public attention while the book underlined the authority of the bishop. The candle, since it could be extinguished, showed that the action could be revoked. The ceremony was held in public during which the bishop and the twelve priests held lighted candles.

He grinned. 'Precisely. Some people afterwards tried to blame me, thought I should have reasoned with the fellow . . . which would hardly made sense at two o'clock in the morning.'

I found Roger Parker remarkable. Yet I could not but feel sorry for him, for all his wealth and eminence a crumpled shadow of his former self.

CHAPTER 19

The making of a vocation . . .

A week later I met Nancy Croft on the High Street. The snow had been cleared away. But it remained bitterly cold.

'A man I wanted to see,' she said. She grabbed my arm. 'It's freezing out here. There's a new milk bar over there. Let's give it a go.'

Milk bars were in vogue, opened by a young couple newly arrived in the town. It was warm. It was glitzy. They were in process of installing a jukebox. I bought her a coffee.

'I hope you'll forgive me for asking,' she said. 'But I'm dying of curiosity. The deviant chaplain wished you a happy circumcision. We've been laughing about it ever since.' She gave my elbow a little sharp nudge. 'But circumcision is close up and personal. And you're a nice looking feller. Does that mean . . .?'

She nodded her head suggestively. I laughed.

'No. He knew I wouldn't agree to it . . . not, I suspect, that he didn't have it in mind.'

I found it surprising. From what I could remember of them, our New Year exchanges had been quite risqué, hence my allusion to Father Tom's Christmas card. We were now stone cold sober, yet she expected the ribaldry to continue.

'The fact remains nevertheless,' I said, 'that Father Tom is probably the most promiscuous parson on earth. The diocese was courting disaster when he was appointed to the chaplaincy. It's a cliché, but it's true. To put him in charge of a male student hall of residence was like giving an alcoholic the keys to the brewery.'

Her face changed. She had been provocative. Now she was deadly serious.

'In that case something must be done about it.'

I clamped my hand on her wrist.

'Don't even think about it. I was a student at the Church Hostel before I went to the theological college. I know what Father Tom is like. He may be footloose, but he will not waylay a student that is not that way inclined.'

This was getting complicated.

'That, though, is hardly the point,' I said. 'Whatever else might be said about Father Tom, his work as chaplain to the university is quite brilliant, beyond the wildest dreams of the diocesan bigwigs that put him there. Without knowing it, they've got it right. He gets through to his student congregation as nobody else . . . though the diocesan authorities would sack him if they knew what he's like. There are some things in life that are best not left to the great and the good.'

She peered into my face sceptically.

'So?'

'It's not at all easy to explain. All I can tell you is what I understand of it.'

That Nancy was intrigued there was no doubt. It was difficult to know where to start.

'I suppose I should begin with "style",' I said. 'I had never really thought about it before. I was a student at Church Hostel at my father's insistence. I resisted the idea, but he hoped I would be ordained. So I attended Father Tom's services. I'm not quite sure why. Perhaps it was out of curiosity, so many people were talking about him. But I found myself presented with a quite different perspective from anything I had ever experienced before.'

I gave her a little smile before continuing, 'You know what the Vicar of Mold is like. He stands at the altar. He says the words. He administers the sacrament. And that is that. But Father Tom's treatment of the liturgy is something else. You might call him high church, but whatever you might think of him, the mass becomes a life-changing missive that is sent forth into the world. The best part of twenty centuries have passed since the church began. There have been conflicts and heresies. But the liturgy has acquired "style", a timeless, all-embracing power and majesty. You could belong to any time or any place when you are there. The vicar wears a surplice and stole. But Father Tom in his vestments is a priest of the most high God. Nothing else matters in the whole wide world.' I gave her a further fleeting smile. 'You can imagine my surprise when I came to Mold and was confronted with the liturgical etiquette of the Elizabethan court.

'And then what happens? We are all immersed in the liturgy when he comes down to the lectern and the sermon begins. And that too is something else. How can I explain it?'

I leaned forwards.

"There is one central point. It's unmissable. Tom's relationship with God is the one fundamental fact of his life, the very essence of his being, as real to him as the air he breathes. The rest of us might prevaricate, but not Father Tom. There's an old adage: Christianity is not taught . . . it's caught. And certainly, you can catch it from him. I was a sceptic, if not a budding atheist, when I first went up to university, fed up with my father's manipulations and sermons. The more he wanted me ordained, the more I resisted it. But Father Tom put an end to that. Nowhere else will you find such a spark with which to ignite the fire of faith.'

Even in retrospect I found it remarkable what Father Tom had done for me.

'But there's a great deal more to it than that. Father Tom turns theology on its head. The Bible speaks of God's almighty power. "Let there be light, and there was light."[52] It's the primary statement of the Old Testament. God's authority is not any the less absolute in the New . . . where he is also seen as a loving father, unlimited power mediated through unbounded love.' I held up my hands. 'But Tom's sermons point to the devastation that is wrought by divine love.'

52 Genesis 1, 3

Nancy stared at my face.

'But it's supposed to be good,' she said. 'Love divine and all that, the vision of perfect bliss at every wedding.'

Like divine intervention, the jukebox came startlingly to life. It was Elvis at his best. His words reverberated in my mind. His hands were shaky, his knees weak the unanticipated èclat of love. I remembered my first encounter with Ann, on the steps leading up to her lodgings near the university. It was a moment. I was thunderstruck. There were kaleidoscopes in my mind. I don't think she even noticed me.

The music stopped as suddenly as it started.

'You see? Elvis is right. You are all shook up. It comes at you from nowhere. No other experience in life can be so shattering. Yet you love it with your very soul.'

There was a spark in Nancy's eye. She had caught the mood.

'It's a long time since I was a teenager,' she said. 'How can I forget it?'

I immediately thought of Rosemary, the girl I had once first loved.

'It's the best thing that has happened in the whole of your life,' I said.

'And then . . . it's the worst moment in the whole wide world when it goes wrong.'

I put my hand on her arm.

'That is the point. If God's invincible power is without limit, so is his desire. Father Tom speaks of a God so obsessed with his craving for the love of mankind that our indifference reduces him to despair. That's why I say he turns theology on its head. "He came into his own," says St John's Gospel, "and his own received him not."[53] But it's catastrophic. The almighty and ever living God who is above all and through all and in us all is reduced to nothing, desirous as no other lover is desirous, spurned as no other lover is spurned.'

I paused to allow her to absorb it, then gave Nancy another smile.

'Father Tom speaks of nothing else. "I am your God. You are my beloved.' I looked into her eyes. (I was worked up. I should have been more careful. I almost, momentarily, meant it.) 'I love you. I have always loved you. I will never abandon my love for you. Am I not your faithful, your ever willing, ever suffering servant? For what other reason would I so excruciatingly have died for you upon the cross? And how do you respond? You don't care. You promise. Yet always you let me down. How can you be so uncaring, so utterly callous?'

I asked, 'Have you read the Book of Hosea?' "And the Lord said to Hosea, Go, take unto thee a wife of whoredoms and children of whoredoms; for the land hath committed great whoredom departing from the Lord."[54]

'It's the ultimate nightmare among the books in the Old Testament. His prophecies are driven by the infidelities of his adulterous wife. She is the ultimate bitch. Never is there a man more in love. Never was he more betrayed. So is God's love unreciprocated by mankind.'

53 John 1, 11

54 Hosea 1, 2b

I stopped for a moment to emphasise the point, before continuing, 'There is no doubting Father Tom's integrity. His sermons come straight from the heart. Their impact is astonishing. The people who flock to hear him in the little chapel at Church Hostel find his preaching riveting.'

Again, I put my hand on her arm.

'Which brings me to the crux of the matter. It's also Father Tom's undoing. On one hand his sermons are awash with "*agape*", the unsullied vision of divine love. Nothing could be more perfect, more absolute. But we can only guess as to what else is happening. He does his utmost to conceal it. Yet there's a frenzy, a madness to him with every sexual conquest he makes. He is the antithesis of St Bernard of Clairvaux whose vision of paradise transmutes the eroticism of *The Song of Songs* into the ultimate perfection of love divine: "You want me to tell you why and in what measure God is to be loved. The reason for loving God is God himself, and the measure is to love without measure." [55]

'But the conflict is within himself. Father Tom is no less sexually driven than the student congregations that flock to hear him. They have that in common. The university is a battlefield between nurture and nature. The students are privileged. Their tuition fees are paid.[56] They receive grants for their lodgings and textbooks, fostered by a society that

55 '*Vultis ergo a me audire, quare et quomodo diligendus sit Deus? Et ego: Causa diligendi Deum, Deus est; modus, sine modo diligere.*'

56 Student loans were introduced under the *Education Act 1962*.

expects their best in return. And then what happens? Nature commandeers them. Their studies are overtaken by a pair of sparkling eyes, driven by instincts as potent as life itself. So what do they do about it? Sublimate it . . . or wreck their futures by procreating a child? You can see the dilemma. The university tries to restrict them, segregating the men and women into single-sex halls . . . which gives rise to a frustrated and difficult generation in which the most inhibited achieve the best degrees.'

They were still tinkering with the jukebox as I went for two more coffees.

'As I was saying, what you hear in Father Tom's sermons and what is really happening are two different things. He keeps his affairs discreet, as you might expect of a priest presenting a divine vision to the world. But I don't think there's any doubt about it. He revels in his sexual exploits. The more prohibited the act, the more it enthrals him. And certainly, he lives dangerously. It is after all illegal.'[57] I raised my hands. 'Yet Sunday by Sunday Father Tom has us transfixed with his vision of a destitute God crying out in vain for our reciprocation of his love. Nor is the drama confined to his sermons, permeating every second of the rite, taking each one of us, it seems, to the very portals of eternity. Nobody celebrates the drama of the mass quite like Father Tom.'

I had thought about these ideas many times.

57 Homosexual relationships were decriminalised under the *Sexual Offences Act 1967*.

'People identify good behaviour with Christian belief,' I said. 'Yet many perfectly good people have no time for religion. It takes a flawed being like Father Tom to bring the faith to life. Nor should we think of Christianity as a moral code. It's a burning passion, a wildfire of the soul.'

I gave it further thought.

'It's not,' I said, 'that Father Tom doesn't feel guilty. Again, I can only speculate. But it seems evident. With every act of illicit love, he betrays his fealty to the God that loves him. That is his dilemma. He loves it. Yet with every bone in his body he loathes the sexual affairs he so palpably adores. I'm reminded of Marlowe's *Faustus* where, in return for earthly pleasures, the protagonist sells his soul to the devil: "O, I'll leap up to my God! Who pulls me down? See, see where Christ's blood streams in the firmament!"[58]

'It's schizophrenic,' I said. 'Father Tom is a living version of Faustus, suspended irredeemably between heaven and hell.'

But Nancy had had enough of it. She took a miniscule sip of her coffee. There was something about her. I could see she was less than impressed.

'It must be wrong,' she said. 'How can he go fucking[59] about all over the place while at the same time spouting out about the love of God? Do what I say, not what I do?

58 Faustus, Act 5, Sc 4

59 The etymology of the word 'fuck' is difficult to establish. While it was undoubtedly common parlance, it was considered too obscene to be put into writing.

It makes him a hypocrite . . . which is exactly what I expect of people who read books. Books overdo everything. There's got to be a drama otherwise nobody would read the ruddy things. To make sense of it you need somebody pig ignorant like me.'

The more I saw of Nancy, the more I liked her.

'I've never had much truck with homosexuals,' she said. 'Their behaviour seems to me to be very rude . . . though I suppose really all sex is rude.' She shook her head. 'But I also didn't have much truck with *The News of the World* when it went over the top a few years ago about that Lord Montague of Beaulieu.[60] The silly buggers charged him with buggery.'

It was her turn to study me.

'But these are the facts as I understand them. I have never set eyes on your Father Tom. He may be gay. I don't believe it sets him apart. You say he does things and then regrets them. That's not schizophrenia. It's the way we all behave. I do wrong. I feel guilty. I forgive myself.' A gleeful expression came into her eyes. 'And if I find it irresistible, I do it all over again.' She gave me a grin. 'Don't believe what it tells you in that play. There's no such thing as the devil. By their nature human beings are entirely mixed up and contradictory. It doesn't mean we're all round the bend.'

60 On 24th March 1954, Edward Douglas Scott-Montague, Peter Wildeblood and Michael Pitt-Rivers were convicted of acts of homosexuality and imprisoned at Winchester Assizes.

She didn't know it, but her words echoed St Paul's: 'For the good that I would I do not, but the evil which I would not, that I do.'[61]

'There's one further point to it,' she said, smiling. 'You don't admit it, but your eyes say it. You owe your vocation to the extraordinary Father Tom.'

It was a moment of truth. But there was a great deal more to it than that. I was sparked off by Tom certainly, but my father also had a great deal to do with it. I remembered those Christmases when my sisters and I were small, when he told us spellbinding stories about the shepherds and the wise men. At that age they were not difficult to believe.

'Give me a child until the age of seven,' says the Jesuit, 'and I will show you the man'. It didn't always have that effect. My schoolfriend John McGrath, the playwright, had long abandoned his parents' staunch Roman Catholicism. But it made me more thoughtful, more pastoral, more concerned with the people in my care, though I was no longer the raw young student that first encountered the intensities of Father Tom.

61 Romans 7, 19

CHAPTER 20

The care of all the churches

I was particularly concerned about the people of New Brighton. Not only was there a rift between them and the vicar, but, from our first encounter, I had taken to them, and they had evidently taken to me. I was always assured of a warm welcome. They had forgiven the fuss I made about the lightbulbs. On many a Sunday afternoon, I joined the organist, John William Faulkner, as we made our way up the hill to Evensong at the church. The main road was not usually so heavily trafficked, but it still sent shivers down my spine when I remembered that first petrifying procession through the village.

So, what could I say about New Brighton? The church had none of the grandeur of St Mary's. But the church is not a building. It's a cliché. The people are the church, in the instance of New Brighton, giving rise to a distinctive society. The organist exemplified the point. He may have rented a house in Mold, but he was born in the village and remained endemically a New Brightonite: an independent, self-made man given to very definite ideas. How he accompanied the services defied credibility. He had never learned to read music.

'It took me a long time to figure it out,' he said. 'I started by having a go on a piano. But it was well worth it.' The thought of it excited him even then. 'The organ is the most wonderful of musical instruments. Nothing produces so great a variety of sounds.'

And certainly, he was a master of the organ at the church: a monster of an electronic Hammond, its main shortcoming the two outsize loudspeakers that were stationed in the sanctuary. I was all but annihilated by them whenever I was at the altar.

'I don't receive any payment,' he said. 'I do my work at the factory. That is how I earn a living. When I play the organ, that is when I live.'

As a trade unionist, not unexpectedly, John was an enthusiastic member of the Labour Party. My own predilections were different. Having been brought up by my father to believe every word that is written in the recalcitrant *Daily Mail*, my education at the Alun School was indebted to a teaching staff made up almost exclusively of left-wing activists from the South Wales valleys. The school was a cave of Adullam[62] in the predominantly Conservative County of Flint. The headmaster, Mr Jeremiah Jenkin[63] was chief among them, and, whenever there was a staff vacancy,

62 1 Samuel 22, 1. David took refuge in a cave near Adullam during his insurrection against Saul.

63 For my sixth form prize, I chose *Collected Poems 1934–52*, by Dylan Thomas. A look of fury came into the headmaster's eye. 'That wretched boy,' he said. He had been Dylan's chemistry teacher.

he made it his business to appoint yet another liberal. So confronted at home and at the school with the conflicting cajoleries of the two main political parties, it seemed best to discard both. Nor, enamoured though I was of Wales, was I prepared to embrace Plaid Cymru. The electoral arithmetic was against it.

The members of the appointments committee to the Mold Borough Council were Labour aficionados. So when he decided to give up industrial disputes, they turned John down for the job of caretaker to the municipal offices in the town. There were two applicants. John appeared before them in a suit, collar and tie. Jerry, the man they appointed, was unwashed, unshaved and in overalls. The stereotype had won the day. But the councillors weren't totally deranged. They sacked Jerry a fortnight later and went on to appoint John. There was a great deal about John to appreciate, but I wondered how much better would he have been were he not so determinedly self-taught?

Nor, when I came to think about it, were the rest of the New Brightonites any less idiocentric. I remembered when I was at school the difference between us and the pupils that were bussed in from nearby Buckley, notable for their strong midlands accents which were not always easily understood. We called them 'the Buckley mugs'. The town's links with the borough of Stoke-on-Trent,[64] which

64 The federation of Stoke-on-Trent was formed in 1910, amalgamating the six towns of the Staffordshire potteries.

went back centuries, begun when it was discovered there were surface coal deposits and hard clay in the vicinity, allowing for the manufacture of pottery. Buckley pots were still on sale, though the industry went into decline in the years before the war. The New Brightonites were linked to the same history. The village was originally called '*Pentre Catherall*', Catherall's village, a name commonplace in the Five Towns. But the Welsh name for devil is '*cythrael*', so the place became known as '*Pentre Cythrael*', the devil's village. By a stroke of genius, it was discarded in favour of New Brighton, the Merseyside holiday resort.

My relationship with the New Brightonites was profound. I found them a remarkable and strange people. Who else would think of burying a dead cat on the crossroads at midnight?

CHAPTER 21

Quite simply, the Teds

But then I was confronted with tribulations of my own. There was the youth club, and there were the Teds. The youth club was underway one Friday evening when the main doors flew open and a dozen of the Teds swaggered in, popinjays in full pomp. It was the last thing I expected. But word must have got round because the quiz promptly stopped, the youth stubbed out their cigarettes and grabbed their belongings. Mindful of her priorities, Rosie collected the record player and the forty-fives. Then the members of the youth club left, streaming up the steps behind the curtains and across the stage, making their way out through the old vestry door at the back. It seemed no more than a matter of seconds before I was left to confront the interlopers. They looked a great deal more intimidating than they had appeared on the street.

'I'm Grimbold,' said the chief Ted . . . at least I thought he was the chief Ted. He was certainly the most prominent. For all his sartorial splendour, his face was ruddy, pockmarked and hardworn. He examined me accusingly. 'And you're the holy Joe.' His voice was nasal, adenoidal. He glanced at the others, then shrugged his shoulders. 'We came to join the youth club, but they're gone, so we'd better help you tidy up.'

A pile of wooden folding tables was stacked against the wall. I was only too conscious of the furnishings, sacrosanct, paid for by the fundraising of the volunteers. He went over, picked one up and threw it. It landed some six yards away, coming apart at as it fell. I tried to intervene. He snatched up another.

'Hey! Wiggy! Catch!'

The table flew, then slithered across the floor. I had no choice but to confront him.

'Please,' I said, 'please, don't do that. You will get me into all sorts of trouble.'

It seemed to please him. The other Teds found it amusing and gathered round. I found myself marooned in the centre of a bullring, the curate versus Grimbold, them to a man against me. I felt sick.

'Look,' I said.

Abruptly, a young, helmeted policeman appeared in the doorway, a look of fury in his eye. He pointed a finger.

'You! Out! Now!'

Nothing could have been more dramatic. The Teds did not argue. They shuffled out, an assortment of dedicated troublemakers with their long multi-coloured coats and glistening DAs. The policeman came over and gave me a grin.

'You're the Reverend Hughes, aren't you?' He nodded his head in their direction. 'I'll say one thing about the Teds. They're a menace if they're allowed, but they know what's good for them. They don't believe in arguing with the police.'

He looked around. 'Nice place you've got here. Handy too. I expect you know the police headquarters is just down the road. It's the county centre for police cadets, so there are plenty of us.' He looked at his watch. 'I must be off. Give us a shout if you have any more problems.'

With that he was gone. The youth club had vanished. There was nothing for it but to clear up the debris and lock up.

I spent a troubled night, after which I joined the vicar to say the office in St Mary's the following morning. Like Elvis I was 'all shook up', but the liturgy must come first. So, I went into the choir vestry under the tower to ring the bell.[65] The allotted psalm seemed to say it all: 'The plowers plowed upon my back: and made long furrows.'[66] There was an old lady in my father's parish who regularly opened the Bible at random, believing that the first words she saw were a sign from the 'good book'. I could not, would not, believe in such delusions.

'It's simply ridiculous,' I said to the vicar afterwards. 'I don't see how I can run a youth club when we're threatened by Teddy Boys.'

He remained unmoved.

'I don't think you need concern yourself about that, Mr Hughes. I suggest you have a word with Mr Hammersley. He will know what is to be done. More importantly, it's time we talked about your forthcoming wedding.'

65 cf *The Book of Common Prayer*, the 'General Rubricks of Morning and Evening Prayer'

66 Psalm 129, 3

A shiver of guilt ran down my spine. Ann thought it was all arranged. We had discussed it at length and expense over the phone. The upshot was simple. As the vicar had pointed out, weddings usually took place at the bride's parish church, but we had found the alternative compelling. So we were to be married at eleven in the morning on 4th April, the Saturday after Easter, in Lady Margaret Beaufort's magnificent parish church of St Mary the Virgin. Yet, apart from setting the date, I had made no further arrangements about it with the vicar. In the event, I need not have worried.

'Do not give the ceremony a moment's thought,' he said. 'I will expect you and your bride to select the hymns. The rest of the arrangements you can leave to me.' There was also a sting in the tail. 'It will be necessary for you to read your own banns.'

Later that week, I poked around the back streets before I could find him, Ron Hammersley, painter and decorator, a diminutive man in tarnished white overalls, up a ladder, paintbrush in hand, a cigarette dangling from the corner of his mouth. He came down to talk to me. He seemed amused.

'The vicar came to see us once,' he said, 'while my wife Val was expecting our third. But I didn't think I'd be bothered by parsons while I'm at work.'

I told him about my problem with the Teddy Boys. He too was not in the least put out.

'OK,' he said. 'I'll be along to the Church Hall on Friday night. Might be a bit late. Got to have a wash, get changed and have a bite to eat.'

I didn't mind what he did so long as he was there to confront the Teds . . . though it was difficult to imagine how he could possibly alleviate the problem.

Friday night came. The youth club came. The Teds came, and, as before, the youth club left. There were even more Teds.

'You can't say we didn't warn you,' Grimbold said. 'We don't think you should get away with it.' He turned to the others. 'Let's give it a go.'

With that, they began wrecking the place, crunching their boots into the tables and chairs, tearing down the curtains, hunting around for anything and everything they could despoil. There was a smashing of glasses and crockery from the kitchen and a crash of cutlery as it was strewn across the floor. I felt helpless. Then . . . it could not have been more dramatic . . . at the height of the mayhem, Ron Hammersley walked in. The Teds were caught amidships. They looked stunned. I found it difficult to believe. He stood in the centre of the hall.

'Can any of you lads fight?'

'Oh no, Mr Hammersley,' one of them said. 'We wouldn't dream of doing anything of the sort.'

He stripped off his jacket and draped it carefully over the back of a chair.

'OK, I'll have six of you.'

It was bizarre. They did exactly what they were told. There was a great deal of discussion. They selected their combatants. Then six of them came at him. The fights outside pubs and dance halls paled into insignificance. For all his smallness,

Ronnie was transformed. He was like a giant spider, bent at the knees, his feet spread wide apart, his body swivelling at the waist, his breath taken in short snorts. In a whirlwind, his fists were picking out the chins of each of his adversaries in turn. It was aggressive certainly. It was as though they were fighting *The Creature from the Black Lagoon*. But it was an aggression finely tuned. They threw themselves at him. They could not come near him, every thrust, every lunge was parried peremptorily away.

'I have to be careful not to hurt them,' he said as he jolted their heads back, thwarting each one of them in turn.

The conflict did not last long. All too soon the Teds were in retreat. I had never before taken the slightest interest in prizefighting. I was fascinated now. But if the Teds were finished, Ronnie was not. He was not even out of breath. He strolled over to talk to them.

'You lads,' he said, 'shouldn't let yourselves be pushed around.'

I cannot begin to describe my sense of relief. Most of the Teds left, but a few others, including Grimbold and Wiggy, stayed on while we spent the rest of the evening discussing how we might set up a boxing club. It seemed the perfect solution. Ronnie had spent three years as a professional, classified as a lightweight.

'I was knocked out of the championship in 1953,' he said. 'It was for the best. I had made enough money to start my own business.' He waved a hand. 'But I have all the gear. My seconds and the rest of the gang are still around. We could set up a boxing club in no time.'

The derelict buildings on the driveway to the vicarage came to mind.

'We could set ourselves up in the old institute,' I said. 'Nothing goes on in there.'

'The club should not be just for the Teds,' Ronnie said. 'Everybody and anybody should be able to join in.'

* * *

Banns were valid for three months. I had made arrangements for them to be read in Ann's parish church. Then, on the following Sunday, Septuagesima, 25th January, I made my announcement at Mattins after the Third Collect: 'I publish the banns of marriage between . . . also between . . . also between . . . also between . . . also between Richard Millree Hughes of this parish and Ann Patricia Stephens of the parish of Christ Church, Bootle . . . also between . . .'

There were several upcoming weddings. I put us mid-list, hoping we could pass unnoticed. There was a strong rustle of amusement among the members of the congregation. Predictably, in the weeks that followed, there was a reduction in the nubile young women that attended the services, though the old ladies continued as before.

CHAPTER 22

Hope springs eternal . . .

I was invited to tea one day by Miss Georgina Prince.

'Your girlfriend Ann is utterly delightful,' she said. 'You were wise to park her with me overnight. We don't want people gossiping.' She poured me a cup of tea. 'But you had her to yourself during the day. I wouldn't hold back if I were you. Have some fun. Let it all hang out. You're only young once.'

Ann was surprised when I told her about it.

'Poor old thing,' she said. 'Perhaps she regrets her own missed opportunities.'

I wasn't sure about that.

'She could,' I said, 'have been quite naughty when she was young.'

* * *

What astonished me was the quantity of equipment required for the setting up of a boxing club. Ronnie's painter and decorator van kept buzzing to and fro as more and more equipment was piled into the rooms of the old institute. The building had its advantages. Since it was unused, we could do more or less whatever we liked. There was no reason why the corner posts of the boxing ring should not be anchored to the floor. I found the structure amazing, as intricate as a spider's web, the stuffed and covered turnbuckles reaching inwards to sustain the padded corners of the ring itself.

'Why is it called a ring when it's a square?' I asked Jim Bradley, formerly Ronnie's manager, a tall swarthy man probably in his late fifties.

He grinned.

'It used to be a ring when they went in for prizefighting in the old days,' he said.

I found the concept strange, nevertheless. The contestants were out to do each other the maximum damage, yet everything was arranged for their protection. The ringside ropes were padded and made taut to stop the opponents from crashing out, while a layer of thick matting underlay the heavy canvass of the floor.

The arrival of the ring was merely the beginning as ever more equipment was delivered to the door. There were several small rooms in the old institute. In one they set up a fig-shaped speed bag, while another accommodated a small double-ended bag attached by cords to the ceiling and the floor. The speed bag was to develop the accuracy of their punches while the double-end bag was to foster a boxer's speed and flexibility. To that was added a sand-filled, heavy bag, indispensable, I was told, for the training of beginners. Some of the fixtures seemed more laughable than serious. My sisters had played with skipping ropes when they were small. But who would have thought that skipping ropes would have their uses for the training of grown men? And why on earth did they need a mirror to admire themselves while shadowboxing?

Not many Teddy Boys turned up on that first Wednesday evening. There was Grimbold and his diminutive friend Wiggy . . . whose name, I discovered, was Jonathan. He was nicknamed in reaction to his scrawny fair hair, incapable of effecting an authentic DA. They both looked incongruous in their long jackets and boots.

'More of us wanted to come,' Wiggy explained. 'But it's not part of the plan. We're never in Mold on a Wednesday.'

To my surprise, the youth club members Ivor and Percy turned up with Rosie and Winnie in tow. They stood around to watch as Jim Bradley emptied out a series of cardboard boxes. He held up a pair of boxing gloves.

'You will be using these,' he said. 'They are not meant for fighting.' He weighed them in his hands. 'They are heavier, meant to be used for training.'

He brought out rolls of cotton hand wrap, gumshields, padded headguards and a further collection of sparring gloves and boots. He put on a headguard.

'Beware,' he said. 'It looks very good. But don't expect it will stop you from being knocked out. A lot of beginners make that mistake.'

I discovered, to begin with, it was not the art of boxing that mattered. We were joined by Ronnie who was anxious to make a start.

'I expected a few more of you,' he said. 'But we might as well get on with it. There are spare chairs in the room next door. Get yourselves one and bring one for me.'

When they were settled, he began.

'I'm not even going to start to teach you how to box. You first need to know what it means.'

That Ronnie was an accomplished storyteller there was no doubt, and he regaled us with his experiences in and out of the ring.

'That Mister Arthur Edwards, the maths teacher when I was at the secondary modern, do you know what he told the class? "Ron Hammersley will be on the dole for the rest of his life." What do you think of that?' It evidently still rankled. 'How dare he say such a thing? But I'll tell you something. I can buy and sell him any time I like.

'Sometimes we would go to a fair in one of the towns,' he said. 'Jimmy would set up a temporary ring. Then he'd get some enormous boxer, the bigger the better, to put up in front of the crowd. There was a chap called Charlie the Bulldozer . . . I never did know his real name. He would walk up and down, shouting, sticking out his belly and waving his fists. I was planted in the crowd. It worked well because I'm not very big. Then the cry would go up. "Who has the guts to fight the champion? There's ten pounds in it if you win." Sometimes we'd get a volunteer. But it always ended up with me.' He nodded his head. 'We took as many bets as we could and, at the end, I'd pretend to knock him out. It wasn't worth enormously big bucks. But it was good for a laugh, and we made more than a few bob.'

He became serious.

'This is the first lesson. You have to learn how to hit an opponent and how not to hit him. Pulling a punch is easy if you know how. You've seen those all-in wrestlers on television? They look as though they're going to kill each other.' He laughed. 'And when the fight is over, they all go off together for a cup of tea.'

Ronnie laid down the rules.

'With skill comes responsibility. A trained boxer will face a load of trouble if things get out of control.'

I tried to determine their reactions. Rosie and Winnie found it exciting. Ivor and Percy were impressed.

'If you change the meetings to a Thursday everybody will come,' Grimbold said.

Although that was when I held my confirmation classes, I found it reassuring. Ronnie's victory over the Teds was not simply a matter of skill over brute strength. He gave serious consideration to the wellbeing not only of the Teds but of any of the others that might come to join the club. It was the beginning of a firm friendship between us, which included his wife, Val. It was quite exciting. I could not wait to introduce them to Ann.

CHAPTER 23

Llanrhaeadr-ym-Mochnant

I was told about it when my mother came for coffee. For some years my father had been Vicar of Cilcain where the parish church had been his pride and joy. The mediaeval hammerbeam roof over the nave rivalled that of the great hall in Hampton Court. The parish was deeply in debt when he was appointed, but after endless fundraisings and economies, the deficit was finally cleared. So, at the instance of the bishop, he was invited to take the incumbency of Llanrhaeadr-ym-Mochnant in south Denbighshire, a village famous for its waterfall[67] some six miles west of the Shropshire border. It was also of great historic interest because in the 1570s and 80s the vicar was the illustrious William Morgan, translator of the Bible into Welsh. Dedicated to Elizabeth I, *Y Beibl Cyssegr Lân* was published in 1588, commemorated in the Cilcain parish records as the year of the Armada.

As we had done years before, I joined the family when we went to inspect the vicarage. We just about fitted into my father's new Ford. My sister Jean was away at the

67 the highest in England and Wales

university, but, since it was a Saturday, Gill and my younger brother Michael were with us. They were excited, while my mother, forever quiet and longsuffering, was sceptical. I was disappointed by my first sight of the house. I had expected something a great deal more historic, but there it was, yet another example of classic Victoriana, stone built with black and white sash windows and a stout oak front door. We were met by the vicar's warden, Mr Percy Evans.

'The clergy are not so well off these days,' he said. 'But they were wealthy in years gone by, so they thought it an honour to add extensions onto William Morgan's house. The front is more recent than the older parts at the back.'

He ushered us through the hallway into the central dining room where the walls are wainscoted and there was a vaulted ceiling.

'This dates back to William Morgan's day. It is thought to have been his study.'

The room was unfurnished but there was a picture of an Elizabethan bishop hanging on the wall to the left of the fireplace. He pointed it out. 'He was afterwards made Bishop of Llandaff, then of St Asaph. But what you see here is the portrait of an imaginary bishop printed in 1907, the work of an Anglesey artist called Thomas Prytherch. We have no likeness of Bishop Morgan himself.'[68] Also, evidently relatively recent, was an imposing black fire surround punctuated at intervals with white marble book

68 In *The Encylopedia Brittanica*, the portrait is treated as authentic.

ends. 'They're a kind of tribute,' he said. 'Some people say he worked at his desk in this room, while others claim he carried out his translation in a cabin in the woods.' Not for an instant could I believe that. William Morgan would have consulted a great many books, papers and manuscripts, many of them irreplaceable, not to be exposed to the elements.

So the history of the house was made clear. While the front parts were the additions of wealthy Victorian vicars, the central room, the cellar and kitchen areas belong to the late mediaeval period. Percy Evans reinforced the point. 'The building has been reoriented. The present house faces north onto the road that runs through the village. But the original house faced south overlooking a track alongside the stream.' We went to inspect the parish church, dedicated to St Dogfan,[69] a long, ramshackle building complete with a blue concave ceiling decorated with stars. The Reverend Silas Evans,[70] a member of the Royal Astronomical Society, was responsible for the stars. But my mother continued to ask questions about the house. 'How many rooms are there?' 'About twenty.' 'They've made the place into a labyrinth,' she said.

'We are full of admiration for him now,' Percy Evans said as we returned to the driveway in front of the vicarage. 'But William Morgan's parishioners thought he was neglecting them, which is hardly surprising when much of his time

69 Martyr, fifth century

70 Vicar, 1909–38

was taken up with the translation. Evidently, they were quite rumbustious about it. He kept a pistol in the pulpit in case matters got out of hand.' He thought a moment. 'That was not the only complication. The Church of England had broken away from the papacy, and the clergy were treated as dogsbodies of the state. It was a period of national crisis with the coming of the Spanish Armada, so he was expected to train the local militia . . . at which he was not very good.'

He chuckled.

'But there were even more problems than that. It's not unusual for the clergy to get themselves into a pickle. He married a woman called Catherine *Ferch*[71] George. So far as I know they were happy. But her mother was a complete harridan. She went out of her way to make the trouble, stoking up a feud between him and Ieuan ap Meredydd, a lawyer from the parish of Llansilin.[72] Mostly, it amounted to a lot of gossip, accusation and counter accusation. It was acrimonious. At one point, Meredydd raised a posse, beat up the vicar's militia and went on to lay siege to the vicarage. I'd have loved to have been here to see that.'

Afterwards, we held a family discussion. My mother remained sceptical, but my father had made up his mind.

71 daughter of

72 It culminated in a hearing before the Court of Star Chamber. William Morgan was vindicated. It renewed his acquaintance with John Whitgift, the Archbishop of Canterbury whom he had known at Cambridge. *Y Beibl Cyssegr* Lân was published in 1588, dedicated to Elizabeth I, paid for with English money, courtesy of William Morgan's mother-in-law.

'It is a privilege to serve in the footsteps of Bishop William Morgan,' he said. 'Beginning with the *Septuagint*[73] and the *Vulgate*,[74] the scriptures were forever being transmuted from one language to another. Translators have always played an important part in the history of the church.' He paused for a moment. 'But there was more to it than that. Origen of Alexandria compiled the first polyglot in the third century, allowing the scholars to compare parallel versions in the different languages, the one against the other. It was followed by the Complutensian Polyglot published in 1520 at Alcala in Spain. You can see why they did it. William Morgan's *Y Beibl Cyssegr Lân* is no exception. Each new translation brings with it a perspective of its own.'

73 Hebrew religious texts were translated into Greek in the third century BC.

74 The Bible was translated into Latin by St Jerome towards the end of the fourth century AD.

CHAPTER 24

Anathema

As directed, we foregathered on Ash Wednesday, 11th February, in St Deiniol's Church, Hawarden, no less neo-Gothic than the Gladstone library but skewed by Edward Burne-Jones' golden, stained-glass nativity in the west window. It seemed a mistake to face east.

'As I pointed out,' said the Rural Dean, 'it is incumbent on us to read "The Commination" on the first day of Lent.'

I had since become acquainted with the text. The anathematising begins: 'Cursed is he that removeth his neighbour's landmark.' It makes the point . . . nothing has changed. The church is never less than attentive when it comes to property and hard cash. Only thereafter does the church denounce violence: 'Cursed is he that smiteth his neighbour secretly.' Though that too I found strange. How could it be done secretly? Surely his neighbour would notice. But the crunch comes at the end with a comprehensive condemnation of the human frailties singled out by the church: 'Cursed are the unmerciful, fornicators and adulterers, covetous persons, idolaters, slanderers, drunkards and extortioners.'

'I have,' said the Rural Dean, 'asked our good fellow priest Albert if he will conduct the service.'

That was the crux of it. Albert was indeed good, a lovely old parish priest, from his earliest childhood nurtured on the Beatitudes of 'The Sermon on the Mount'. It did not occur to him to do otherwise. So, quite simply, he blessed them: 'Blessed is he that removeth his neighbour's landmark . . . Blessed is he that smiteth his neighbour secretly.'

The choicest was reserved for the last, a comprehensive beatification of unbridled reprobate behaviour. Blessed are 'the unmerciful, fornicators and adulterers, covetous persons, idolaters, slanderers, drunkards and extortioners'. I was kneeling near the back, relishing the heaving shoulders of my fellow clergy as they did everything they could to suppress their mirth . . . though, in terms of pure Christian charity, I think, the lovely old Albert had got it right.

But Ash Wednesday marked the beginning of Lent, the forty days and forty nights of solitary self-denial and prayer trialled by Jesus in the Judean wilderness before the launching of his ministry: 'And when he had fasted forty days and forty nights, he was afterward an hungered.'[75]

The long days and nights of deprivation had taken their toll, their impact hallucinatory, as Nancy would have it, leading Jesus into thinking he was being tempted by the devil. He found it illuminating nevertheless, specifying the errors he must preclude in the pursuit of his ministry. Never should he do evil that good might ensue. Finally, according

75 Matthew 4, 2

to St Matthew, 'angels[76] came and ministered to him'. . . he was probably rescued by desert nomads.

For my own part, I decided to give up smoking during Lent, which rendered me difficult and short tempered, worsened by the fact that the fasting was discontinued on Sundays in honour of the resurrection. My struggles lasted only two weeks. The return of revived withdrawal symptoms each Monday morning was more than flesh and blood could stand.

The following week I received an appointment to take my driving test through the post. 'By all means use the Sprite,' Roger said when I told him about it. 'You've nothing to worry about. You're a very good driver.'

It was his first and only comment on my progress. When I mentioned it to the vicar, he was not so sanguine.

'I think you might have a problem,' he said.

I knew what he meant, though I found it difficult to believe. A few weeks earlier, the Reverend Gerry Rathbone, designated my father's successor as Vicar of Cilcain, had hit the headlines, his crime featured in newspapers all around the world. 'VICAR SLUGS TESTER' was blazoned across the *Chicago Tribune*. On failing to pass his driving test for the sixteenth time, he lost his temper and hit the examiner over the head with the starting handle . . . for which he was given a custodial sentence.

76 An angel, in New Testament terms, is a stranger that brings you good news.

'But driving examiners aren't stupid,' I said. 'They can't think that all clergy are the same.'

'I suggest nevertheless you refrain from wearing a clerical collar,' the vicar replied. 'You might be confronted with the same man.'

He accompanied me when I drove down to Wrexham Street to take to take the test. The examiner, a tall, grey-haired man with a clip board under his arm, asked to see my appointment card . . . which was addressed to 'The Revd'. Immediately, my cover was blown.

'I would be grateful, sir,' the examiner said to the vicar, 'if you would act as an observer during the course of this examination. But I must forewarn you: if at any time you say one solitary word, the exercise will be rendered void and Mr Hughes will be failed. Is that understood?'

The vicar took a seat in the back of the Hillman. The only time he nearly said anything was when I made a rather spectacular emergency stop. Apart from that the exercise went well. For the only time ever, the Sprite did not shudder when it was put into reverse.

That, though, was but the half of it. The examiner turned to the vicar.

'I would be obliged, sir, if you would leave the vehicle.'

As soon as he was gone, he returned his attention to me.

'I've seen some atrocious examples of driving in my time, but yours was positively the worst. You were far too cautious, hanging around, wasting time instead of getting on with it. And your emergency stop was exactly what should not happen on the road. What we need are firmly applied brakes, not some catastrophic full stop.' He gave me a glare. 'Who taught you? Who gave you driving lessons?'

I was obliged to admit it. I was self-taught. The inquisition went on for some time. I wondered why. It seemed evident I had failed.

'Well,' he said at last, 'I cannot do other than to issue you with a pass, Mr Hughes.' He shook my hand. 'May I wish you well on the road in the years to come.'

So . . . he had gone out of his way to rile me. But why? Was he trying me out? If so, he had chosen the wrong man. Also, in that respect, I was not exactly prepared. The Sprite had a starting handle, but I had no idea where it was kept.

These were the disruptions as our Lenten observances continued. At other times, the vicar and I were alone when we said the Daily Office. Now we were joined by a number of devout parishioners.

CHAPTER 25

The devil is in the detail

On 21st February, Ann was back at her home in Bootle for half term. It was magical as before when we met in Liverpool the following Tuesday afternoon. She was full of the latest, regaling me with the behaviour of her headmistress, Miss Hermione Blossom, a strange old dame, the spitting image of Margaret Rutherford.

'It's quite outrageous,' Ann said. 'She owns the school lock stock and barrel, which means she can do exactly what she likes. So what's the latest? She has the matron hard at it with a sewing machine. All the girls, no matter what their age, must wear their skirts at least six inches above the knee.' She grinned. 'They look like randy pelicans.' She thought a moment. 'But Miss Blossom is strict in other ways. The girls are not allowed anywhere near the beach.'

Such were the eccentricities of a girls' private school.

We wandered around the shops. Soon after six we drifted into one of the bars. Ann's tastes had become quite exotic. I bought her a cocktail called Singapore Sling. She had her own Black Sobranie cigarettes.

'Miss Blossom doesn't like her staff going into pubs,' she said. 'She thinks pubs are vulgar. Isi and I gave her the slip one evening and went down to The Brockley Hall Hotel. It's a bit posh. But I thought, what the hell?'

I could envisage her part in it. Her friend Isobel was not one to kick over the traces.

'We met a student in the bar called Diane,' Ann said. 'Her parents manage the hotel. She's reading anthropology and archaeology at Durham. They're into ancient Middle Eastern texts.'

A provocative look appeared in her eye.

'It's the way to explain the origins of religion, the delusions of a primitive civilisation. It's obvious, really. That's how mythology came about. The world was a frozen wasteland during the Ice Age. Then there came a global thaw in about 9000 BC. Nature came to life. The rivers began to flow in the Middle East, culminating in a fertile crescent linking the Nile Valley through the Levant to the alluvial plains of Mesopotamia. Life was transformed with the plenitude of the river valleys. It was the beginning of society, the cradle of civilisation. People had enough to eat and time on their hands. So, they wondered who they were and what their lives were about . . . which gave rise to the creation legends and much else.'

She studied my face.

'Diane talked about it at length. It explains the mythology of the early Old Testament. What do you know about Noah and the ark?'

It amused me, reminiscent of our lectures at the theological college about Genesis in particular.

'Virtually the same tale is told,' I said, 'in Babylonian mythology, *The Epic of Gilgamesh*, where the protagonist is called Utnapishtim. But it's rather more fanciful than the account as it appears in the Bible. Instead of filling it with animals two by two, he made the ark into a giant kindergarten in which to save their infant progeny from the flood.'

I gave her a grin and said, 'Imagine all those little monkeys. The mediaeval miracle plays go on about the gossipy Mrs Noah. But Mrs Utnapishtim must have been driven round the bend.'

It was a serious thought, nevertheless.

'The writers of the Old Testament may have acquired the legend from the Babylonians, but it's treated differently in Genesis,' I said. 'The God of Israel is the prime mover, sending the flood to wreak vengeance on the evil doers of the day. But Noah is a just man, inspired to build an ark to rescue not only himself and his family but the whole animal kingdom. It didn't occur to the myth makers that some creatures don't require saving . . . the fish, for instance, to say nothing of the crocodiles and hippos.'

She nodded.

'Diane talked about that.'

'But the Noah story,' I said, 'is not entirely fictitious. There's good archaeological evidence that there really was an enormous prehistoric flood in the valley of the Tigris and Euphrates.'[77]

77 *Ur of the Chaldees*, Leonard Wooley, 1929, 31

Again, I was amused.

'Sometimes the Old Testament changes the meaning of a legend: 'And Abel was a keeper of sheep, but Cain was a tiller of the ground.'[78] It reminds me of the song in *Oklahoma* where 'The farmer and the cowman should be friends' because there was a rivalry between them. But do you know how the legend originates? It comes from ancient Sumer where Dumuzi, the shepherd god, and Enkimdu, the farmer god, are both in love with Inanna, the love goddess. Which do you think the lady will choose: the wild desert sheik or the trusty, reliable farmer?'

Ann laughed.

'She'll have the sheik, infinitely more romantic.'

'Exactly. But what happens when the story appears in the pages of the Old Testament? The love goddess disappears. There's only one god, the God of Israel. The shepherd and the farmer are reduced to ordinary men. They have an argument about their respective sacrifices: 'And it came to pass, when they were in the field, that Cain rose up against Abel his brother, and slew him.'[79] It was done in a fit of jealousy. The legend began as a rivalry between two suitors. It ends with the world's first murder.'

'It still makes the point,' she said. 'Legends provided the basis for religious belief.'

78 Genesis 4, 2a

79 ibid 4, 8b

CHAPTER 26

Bishop Richard Davies

But that was not the end of it. The following week in the Flintshire County Library on Chester Street, I came across a *Letter to the Welsh from the Right Reverend Father in God Richard Davies, DD, Bishop of St David's.*[80] It was a later edition. The original was written in 1567 as an introduction to an earlier translation of *The New Testament* into Welsh, largely the work of an Oxford scholar called William Salesbury. I knew something of it, but the Salesbury translation had seemed unimportant since, some twenty years later, it was superseded by William Morgan's *Y Beibl Cyssegr Lân*. I thought again about the various books and manuscripts that surrounded him. The Salesbury translation[81] must have been among them.

On the other hand, Bishop Richard Davies' pastoral letter turned out to be of quite inestimable importance. The more I read of it, the more engrossed I became, particularly in the second part where he writes: 'I want there to be a revival

80 *Llythur y Gwir Barchedig Dad yn Nuw Rysiart Dafies, D.D.Esgob Ty Ddewi at a Cymry*

81 *Testament Newydd ein Arglwydd Iesu Christ*

of the ancient catholic faith.'[82] It seemed extraordinary. The church was separated from the traditional catholicism[83] of the church of Rome. I made a point of finding out about Bishop Richard Davies.[84] His father was a Catholic priest called Dafydd ap Gronw,[85] curate to the parish of Gyffin, southeast of Conwy on the North Wales coast. What about his vows? A Catholic priest had fathered a son. But it was not so scandalous as I thought. On the payment of a fee, the Welsh bishops of the period allowed the clergy to keep a woman with the status of wife.

Her name was Sioned. They must have had money because Richard was educated at New Inn Hall,[86] Oxford, where he received his MA in 1530 and BD in 1536. Also, while he was at the university, he embraced Protestantism which, on the accession Queen Mary[87] in 1553, sent him into exile on the continent. Thereafter, following the crowning of Elizabeth I in 1558, he was made Bishop of St David's where, at his palace in Abergwili, he collaborated with Salesbury in his

82 *'dymuno adnewyddiad yr hen ffydd gatholig'*

83 the word means 'universal'

84 1505–81

85 The patronymic naming system of the Welsh was replaced under the *Laws of Wales Acts*, 1535–42.

86 later merged with Balliol College

87 Mary was determined to restore the country to Roman Catholicism.

work as a translator. [88] From so determinedly protestant a background, why was he looking for a revival of the 'ancient catholic faith'?

Richard Davies wrote to his compatriots with deep affection: 'Arouse yourselves once more you lovely Welsh, my beloved and kindly brother in Jesus Christ: don't despair, don't be cast down, don't look at the ground.'[89] He linked their provenance to the earliest appearance of Christianity in Britain when 'in the thirtieth year after Christ's resurrection there came to this kingdom the distinguished senator Joseph of Arimathea, a disciple of Christ, and with him other notable disciples of Christianity'.[90] He mentioned, too, Les ap Coil, the legendary King Lucius who was also credited with bringing Christianity to Britain. While Richard Davies was indebted to what would be considered mediaeval folklore, there is evidence of the early arrival of the Christian faith on these shores.[91] But he was also not impressed, some three centuries later, by St Augustine's mission to the Anglo-Saxons. As he put it:

88 Richard Davies translated 1 Timothy, Hebrews, James, 1 and 2 Peter. Thomas Huet, the precentor, translated Revelation.

89 *'Deffro dithau bellach Gymro glan, fy anwyl a'm caredig frawd yn Nghrist Iesu: paid a'th ddigenhedlu, paid a'th ddifrawi, paid a'th edrych i'r' llawr.'*

90 *'yn y ddegfed flwyddyn ar hugain ar ol dyrchafiad Crist.y death i'r deuyrnas hon sendeddwr anrhydys Joseph o Arimithea, disgybl Crist, ac eraill disgyblion crist'nogaeth dysgedig gyd ag ef.'*

91 The Celtic Church sent representatives to the Synod of Arles in 314 AD.

> *. . . hence the great difference between the Christianity of the Britons and the Christianity Augustine brought to the English. The Britons kept their Christianity pure and unsullied, without mixing it with human considerations, as they had received it from Joseph of Arimathea, Christ's disciple, while the beliefs of Rome hardly took any notice of God's law.* [92]

That was at the heart of it, explaining why he wanted 'a revival of the ancient catholic faith' where the man-made edicts of Rome were not allowed to overtake the unsullied ordinances of God.

How did I feel about it? As in the story of Noah, there was factual evidence at the heart of the mythology. Perhaps rightly the Church in Wales was made a separate province in 1914. So could it not presage the restoration of the 'ancient catholic faith' that Bishop Richard Davies had advocated, freeing the Welsh from the machinations of an egotistical King Henry VIII in headlong pursuit of his divorce? What appealed to me most was the freedom implicit to the heritage of the Celtic saints, their lack of an intrusive discipline imposed upon them from above. I thought about my own beginnings, enmeshed within the unyielding hierarchy

92 *'cyd bai gwahan mawr rhwng Crist'nogath y Brytaniaid at eilun Crist'nogaeth a ddug Awstin i'r Saeson. Y Brynaniaid a gadwasent ei Crist'nogaeth yn bur ac yn ddilwgr, heb gymmysg dychymygion dynol, fel y derbyniasant gan Joseph or Arimithea, disgybl Crist, a chan eglwys Rhufain pan oedd bur yn glynu wrth reoledigeath Duw.'*

of the church. Their faith was not so curtailed. As Richard Davies had pointed out, their allegiance was to divinely appointed laws, not to some trivia brought in by the ecclesiastical establishment.

CHAPTER 27

The moving finger writes . . .

Lent begins with one motif and ends with another. Palm Sunday signalled the change as Jesus' desert preparations gave way to the final dire sequence of his crucifixion and death. A hymn marks the turning point:

Ride on, ride on in majesty!
Hark! All the tribes hosanna cry.
O Saviour, meek, pursue your road
With palms and scattered garments strowed.[93]

There were further changes on the Monday of Holy Week. The time of Morning Prayer was changed to seven thirty to allow for a protracted service of the Holy Communion at eight. Each of the Gospels on successive days tells the story of Christ's trial and crucifixion . . . making the account of it exhaustively long. People usually stood for the reading of the gospel, but the more elderly among us were obliged to take a pew.

93 HH Millman, *Hymns*, 1827

For Ann it was the end of term, marking the completion of her responsibilities at the school. Miss Blossom presented her with a copy of George Orwell's *Animal Farm.*

'You will love this, my dear, so pastoral, gentle and uplifting,' she said.

Afterwards, Ann returned to her home in Bootle with one thought in mind. She needed to buy a bridal dress. Then, in a last-minute change of plan, she decided to come to Mold on Maundy Thursday where she stayed with the Hammersleys overnight. The wedding reception was to be at the flat and Val wanted some decisions on how it was to be done. Ronnie and I joined them that evening for a drink. Their plans presaged a simple affair with wine, *petits fours*, a wedding cake and no great long speeches. I wondered if the last of these could be achieved.

Then came Good Friday with its contemplation of the *Via Dolorosa*, the Way of the Cross. 'Is it nothing to you, all ye that pass by? behold, and see if there be any sorrow like unto my sorrow . . .'[94]

It was a solemn moment followed by Easter Day when there were crowds at all the services. A rubric[95] in *The Book of Common Prayer* stipulates: 'And note, that every Parishioner shall communicate at least three times in the year, of which Easter is to be one.' That people took it seriously there was no doubt. There were three celebrations of the

94 Lamentations 1, 12a, from the Latin '*Surrexit Christus hodie*' A&M, 99

95 They were originally printed in red.

Holy Communion at St Mary's, two at St James and one in the old school at Gwerymynydd. I followed the vicar around to these services, at each reading the epistle and assisting with the administration of the sacrament. There was a triumphant feel to it, epitomised by the exuberance of the hymns:

Jesus Christ is risen today, Alleluia!
Our triumphant holy day, Alleluia![96]

But it was the following Saturday that finally came to occupy my mind. In the presence of our families, friends and a multitudinous crowd of parishioners, Ann and I were married at eleven in St Mary the Virgin's Parish Church on Saturday 4th April 1959. Roger was there, trundled in his wheelchair by Mrs Wright. As he had predicted, the vicar did not stint on the ceremony. Before me was the choir and an array of clergy, presided over by the bishop in full regalia, my father, the vicar, the rural dean and members of the chapter.

Then, to Wagner's *Bridal March*, in a glittering white dress and a floating cloud-like veil, Ann came to stand beside me at the chancel step. There could not have been a greater contrast between us. I was inured to weddings. She was shivering like a leaf. She turned. Our eyes met. The world changed. The choir sang. The bishop pronounced us man and wife.

96 translated in the *Lyrica Davidica*, 1708

There were photographs and much excitement followed by the reception at the flat.

So, I was given to her and she was given to me.

CHAPTER 28

. . . and having writ moves on

We were booked at The Ship Inn at Aberdaron, the last of the fishing villages on the Llyn peninsula where the sacred island of Bardsey lies offshore. I was looking forwards to the intimacy of our honeymoon. But that was not all. Nowhere was more evocative of the ancient Celtic Church than this land. What did Bishop Richard Davies say? 'The Britons kept their Christianity pure and unsullied.' When I mentioned it to Ann, she became quite brusque.

'Can't you, for once, think of something more interesting?'

But Christianity was not the only religion imported into Britain at that time. A temple to the mystery god Mithras was discovered under the site of the Bloomberg building in London.[97] There were parallels between the two faiths. Mithras descended to earth on 25th December to the discomfiture of a company of shepherds.

But first there was our journey to be made. My aunt had lent me her little beige Ford Popular, as Roger Parker had

97 It was discovered in 1954.

it, noisy and, as I discovered, without a heater. But nothing could detract from the pleasure of the moment. Ann looked like a Parisian model in a crisply tailored off-white jacket and dress. I could not have been more proud of her. She may have been an accomplished mathematician, but she was also an unsurpassed needlewoman.[98] The guests at the wedding made a fuss of us as we left. I drove down the road before removing the 'just married' signs and a collection of pendant tin cans.

'I'm starving,' Ann said.

The reception at the flat had been frenetic, too animated to allow either of us to eat. So I pulled in at The Druid Inn in Llanferres where we ordered a meal. We were alone at last . . . only to be intruded upon by the angry growling of a dog, strange because there was no such animal in sight. Then we discovered it was perpetrated by a large grey parrot in a cage. So Ann fed the bird pickled onions . . . which it liked.

I made a diversion off the road between Bala and Trawsfynydd, taking us north over the Migneint, the largest area of blanket bog in Wales inhabited solely by sheep. The road was narrow and meandering, skirting a little stone round-arched bridge in the moorland, which, for no good reason, leads over a stream. I knew the mountain road well from my childhood as it was part of our journey when we visited my grandmother at Llanystumdwy. But I chose it

98 When we were students, she designed and set up a group to make the costumes for a production of Shakespeare's *Measure for Measure*.

with another thought in mind. When I was seventeen, I spent time in Paris, staying with my penfriend, Jean Chevallier, and his widowed mother in a flat near Porte d'Italie. Nothing could have done more to change the direction of my life. When I was five, I picked up Welsh from the children in the playground at the primary school. I studied French at the Alun School in Mold. But when I was in Paris, what taught me Welsh taught me French, learning as an infant learns, given to no other thought than the issue of the moment.

That was not my only instance of wonder. When we visited the Louvre, I was stunned by the enigma of the *Mona Lisa*. I knew what to expect, but still it was astonishing. The picture is so small . . . this was the most famous painting in the world. I had a postcard of her in the car. As we began to descend into the Vale of Ffestiniog, where the river in the distance meanders between uplands before it gently makes its journey to the sea, I showed Ann the postcard.

'It's a cliché,' I said. 'Everybody knows the picture. But look at her. The scenery reflects the complexity of her dreams. Then compare it to what you see of the Dwyryd estuary. Does it not convey precisely the same thoughts?'

It was dazzlingly romantic. For years it had intrigued me. I could almost have thought that Leonardo had been there.

The staff at The Ship could not have been more welcoming. We were given a bedroom overlooking the street. Also, we were forewarned. We would be expected to take second helpings at every meal. They made a point of it. It was their speciality. They were proud of the quality of their cuisine. We went into the bar.

'I would like to visit Bardsey,' I said. 'It would mean a great deal to me.'

'I thought it might,' she giggled, then shrugged her shoulders. 'I know what you're like. You had it in mind all along.' She laughed again. 'I don't see why not. It's your honeymoon as well as mine.'

Later, I asked the manager how we could cross to the island. His answer was frustratingly vague.

'Mr Guto Jones has a farm on Enlli,' he said. 'He comes over to the mainland sometimes. We'll make arrangements for you when he does.'

But there was a magic to the village. We inspected Y Gegin Fawr,[99] a primeval cruck house,[100] the final staging post in the Middle Ages for pilgrims as they neared their journey's end. Two pilgrimages to Bardsey were considered the equivalent of one to Rome. We spent a profligate honeymoon night and, the following morning, attended the Holy Communion at the church of St Hywyn,[101] where I received the sacrament. Afterwards, we wandered down to the sea. It was cold, but the air was fresh and clean. Bardsey cannot be seen from the heavily pebbled beach at Aberdaron, so we returned to the hotel for breakfast then

99 The Big Kitchen

100 using a frame of naturally curved timber

101 Abbot of Bardsey in the sixth century

took the road up onto the headland. And there it was at last.

I thought Ann might find it amusing.

'Father Tom took a group of students on a pilgrimage to the island last year. It was officially arranged. He was given permission to use a deserted manse belonging to the Calvinistic Methodists. There's even a derelict chapel where he could say mass. And somebody lent him a cine camera.' I gave her a grin. 'A few weeks later, when the film was developed, he laid on a party at the Church Hostel and invited their parents to come to see it. I was not there. I was told about it later by my friend Robert Glynne. The viewfinder on the camera was out of kilter. The only things he filmed were bottoms, male and female bottoms, sitting, standing, jogging, climbing into boats, struggling up cliffs . . . you could take your pick.'

Ann was never averse to a little rudery.

'He made a complete arse of it,' she said . . . which would not, I thought, go down well with the Mothers' Union.

CHAPTER 29

They that go down to the sea in ships . . .

We decided that afternoon to make paintings of the island. Nothing could have better illustrated the differences between us. It was crossing a new threshold. We were getting to know each other all over again.

The sun was shining as we went up onto the headland. The sound between the island and the mainland was serene, though it's known for its perfidy where the two seas meet. We went to where the grassland gives way to the rocks. It was not the most interesting prospect of the island, dominated by Mynydd Enlli,[102] a rounded mountaintop rising solidly out of the sea. What was striking was the difference between our two pictures as they appeared. At school I was taught to make colourwashes, allowing the paints to flow translucently down the page. Ann's painting was meticulous, precisely representing every detail she saw. It was unsurprising. No wonder she cut her dress patterns faultlessly.

102 Bardsey Mountain

'I want to spend a night on the island,' I said as we returned to the car. 'It would mean a great deal to me.'

She stopped.

'But that would mean leaving the hotel. Where on earth would we stay?'

'It will only be for one night. There's a tent in the boot of the car. The hotel will supply us with a packed meal.'

She stared at me.

'You seem to have thought of everything. What happens if I don't want to come?'

I shrugged my shoulders.

'Then I'll give up the idea.'

'Won't it be cold if we stay overnight in a tent?'

I laughed.

'I know of a worse predicament. There's a story that the magician Merlin is entombed on Bardsey in a giant sarcophagus of ice.'

That did it. She grinned.

'I simply can't bear the cold. We'd better go over and let him out.' Suddenly she became serious. 'All right. If it means that much to you, of course I will come.'

There was news for us when we arrived back at the hotel.

'I exchanged messages with Mister Guto Jones via the lighthouse,' the manager said. 'He will on the beach at six thirty tomorrow morning. He is coming to sell fish and to collect some nets. He won't hang around. If you're not there, he will leave without you.'

Ann and I were out early, dressed in warm jumpers and anoraks, travelling as lightly as possible with a rucksack, sleeping bags, a bucket and the tent. Guto Jones arrived soon after from the sea, making use of the swell as he hauled his boat up onto the beach. He had several metal bins packed with fish and a number of battered green petrol cans.

It was the boat that particularly drew my attention, wide bodied, about forty feet long, the woodwork scored and pitted through its age-old encounter with the sea. The ensemble seemed primitive, with the engine fitted amidships while a shaft ran away to drive the propeller at the stern.

'*Bore da gyfeillion*,'[103] said the newcomer, a broad-shouldered man in waders and a voluminous grey sweater.

'I'm sorry,' I replied, 'Ann doesn't speak Welsh.'[104]

He nodded. His English was hesitant, making an emphatic use of the consonants.

'You can call me Guto.' He smiled and took Ann's hand. 'A very warm welcome to Enlli. I understand you are newly married.'

A horse and cart with two men came towards us down the beach. We were introduced to Emrys and Hywel. They exchanged cargoes with Guto, replacing his fish bins with empties to which were added fishing nets and a mass of other equipment. They also replaced his petrol cans. But that was the peace before the storm as, with much agitated shouting

103 'Good morning, friends.'

104 *'Mae hi'n ddrwg gen i . . . Ydi Ann ddim yn siarad Cymraeg.'*

and bargaining, they set about calculating how much money was owed to whom. (Why were such transactions so much noisier in Welsh? When she first came to Wales, my mother thought everybody was quarrelling.) Eventually, they shook hands. I paid the fare and they helped us stow our luggage aboard. They pushed us out. Guto pull-started the motor and we were off, belching clouds of acrid blue fumes as we chuntered out into the bay.

The weather was early morning cold, but the sun was shining and the waters were quiet. When we rounded the point as Bardsey came into view, the waves were appreciatively higher. It was alarming in one respect. For the most part, Guto sat in the stern, smoking and manning the tiller. But there came a moment when he abandoned the boat to the waves, his pipe sparking in the wind as he tramped down amidships to tip more petrol into the tank. Nothing could have been more incendiary, though he must have done the same thing a thousand times before. Ann clung to me. I could see the fear in her eyes.

'There's a leak in the tank,' he explained, raising his voice above the elements. 'It's nothing to worry about. I will solder up the hole when I'm not so busy.'

The voyage was nevertheless fascinating as we skirted the bare flanks of Mynydd Enlli, which rose formidably out of the sea, the sun glinting on the waves, the gulls flying and crying while colonies of puffins[105] stood in solemn assembly

105 Bardsey is notable for a variety of puffin called the 'Manx Shearwater'.

on the rocks. There are many colonies of birds on Bardsey, cloughs and oystercatchers, razorbills and shags. Guto abandoned the tiller again to come and stand over us, the boat surging and cresting as he pointed towards the land.

'This part is what they call the observatory,'[106] he said. 'Scholars come here specially to study the birds. They want to know where they are coming from and to where they are going.'

Later, the mountainside fell sharply away, revealing a long, low-lying peninsula stretching away into the sea. There, beyond an isthmus, was the lighthouse.

There was neither pier nor jetty where we came to land. I took off my shoes, strung them by their laces around my neck, rolled up my trousers and lowered myself into the waves. The seabed fell sharply away. It took me by surprise. I was soaked to the waist as I struggled towards the shore. But Guto manoeuvred the boat up against the rocks. He was amused.

'I'd get off here, Mrs Hughes, if I were you.'

She needed no second invitation. He turned to me.

'I will bring your luggage off, Mr Hughes. I don't think you need bother with your tent. You can stay, like the other lot, in the old minister's house. Very likely you should ask the permission of the chapel elders. But I won't say a word. Nobody will know you're there.'

Ann grabbed the bucket and disappeared into the bushes. I took a pair of trousers and a sweater out of the rucksack

106 The Bardsey Bird and Field Observatory was founded in 1953.

and proceeded to follow suit. A girl appeared as I emerged, aged about sixteen or seventeen, broad-faced, smallish, with a mass of jet-black hair. There was something overtly suggestive about her, neo-Gothic, almost Beardsleyish.

'This is my daughter Iona,' Guto said. He laughed. 'You must say her name straight, not like the Scottish island that is spelled the same way. She doesn't speak English.'

Ann reappeared at the same time.

'You've forgotten the bucket,' I said.

She smiled and said, 'I'm sorry. It needs washing out.'

Guto's daughter was nervous as I took her hand. With her was a plump Welsh cob, short-tailed, with the harness already in place.

Her father turned to the girl, '*Tyrd a fo ymlaen*.'[107]

A small cart was standing nearby. He raised the shafts as she backed the horse in.

'There's a stream near the old minister's house,' he said. 'You can see to everything there. I would get on with it if I were you. All you do is follow the track. I will bring you some fish a little later on.'

107 'Bring him forwards.'

CHAPTER 30

Enlli

At first the wayside was a jumble of brambles, celandines, and extensive clumps of stinging nettles. But there were also magical stretches of bluebells flowing away into the woods. I sensed it immediately.

'This is the land as it was a million years ago,' I said, 'as nature intended, untouched by human hand.'

Ann was more analytical.

'Nature makes its own rules,' she said, 'sustaining the life support system.'

There was a sudden flurry as a pheasant flew out of the bushes.

'Look at that bird. The instinct is inbred. It flies. It feels hungry. It forages for food,' she said. 'Have you ever watched a calf being born? Within minutes it's on its feet and ready to suckle.

'We ignore such things at our peril,' she said excitedly. 'People are careless. They do what they like. They tear up the countryside, drain the marshes and swamps. We belong to a throw away culture. If we have no use for something we dump it in the bin.' She shook her head. 'There's a lesson to be learned. Nature recycles everything. A dead rabbit is not left to rot. It's picked over within moments by the carrion crows.'

She became quite serious.

'I believe in a universal web of being in which every living creature plays its part. It's true of your body. Without the microbes in your stomach, you could not digest your food. That is just a hint of it. We may not know how, but even the smallest beetle will make its impact on the world. We act against nature at our peril. The time will come when we will take it too far, when catastrophe threatens and the planet itself will begin to die.'

I laughed.

'It's too Wordsworthian for words,' I said. 'Nature is red in tooth and claw. Do you know what Herbert Read said about Wordsworth? He'd be cured with a week in the jungles of Borneo.'

But the island was not wholly uncultivated. Soon we came across a small farm surrounded by dry-stone walling and long low barns. To one side was an apple orchard.[108] There were fields occupied by languid black cows.

'I'm not stupid,' she said. 'Of course, we must farm the land, but it has to be done with a proper respect.'

Further on, a tall modern crucifix announced the most famous burial place in Wales, reputedly the graveyard of twenty thousand saints of the Celtic Church whose remains were returned to Enlli for burial. There was nothing to see,

108 Bardsey Apples are indigenous to the island.

merely a piece of unkempt ground while the residual ruins of the monastery stood to the left, a survival from the days of the Austin canons. For all its nondescript character, it was the graveyard that was important, evidence of the heyday of the Celtic saints. Many times I had tried to envisage them, masters of the spiritual life, the nearest I could find to my religious ancestors.

'Nothing,' I said, 'could be more unlike the pseudo monasticism of my theological college, regulated like clockwork every moment of every day. The ancient saints were free. They came here to grow in the faith, women as well as the men.'

Ann looked puzzled.

'They don't sound very exciting to me.'

'They're the people of my dreams,' I replied. 'Wandering stars, prophets and poets who made unplanned journeys to found churches wherever they might arrive.' I looked around. 'But this was their mystical home.'

Ann found it funny.

'Some of them, from what I've heard, were pretty crazy. They had a habit of jumping into lillyponds. A woman called Michaela was the patron saint to hares.'

'You mean St Mehangell,' I said. 'Her shrine is at Pennant, not far from Oswestry.'

Ann was undaunted. I was not entirely surprised. She was always a match for me.

'That,' she said, 'is utter twaddle, made up at a later date. I know only what you have told me about the Celtic saints, which isn't very much . . . because I suspect there isn't very much to tell. You should not be deluded by the romance of long ago and far away, as though things were somehow different at some unspecified time in the past. You must learn to face reality. Even if it were true, you cannot be like the Celtic saints. You're not, nor ever can be, what you call free.'

She put a hand on my arm.

'My darling Richard, you're given a lot of leeway as curate of Mold. There are not so many rules compared to the theological college. But the fact remains. You have sworn obedience to the bishop. You're a tiny cog in the hierarchy of the church.'

I was affronted.

'We were told when I was at theological college that the bishops are the chosen ones fulfilling the roles of the apostles of old. But it doesn't have to be like that. I have my vocation. The bishop has his. It doesn't mean that his is more important than mine.'

She gave me a little provocative smile.

'Oh, my darling Richard, I think it does.'

That was Ann. I was forever trying to assess her. She remained an enigma nonetheless, intellectually rigorous, sexually volcanic, but she was not to be diverted.

'The more I think about it,' she said, 'the more sceptical I become.' She looked around. 'Don't misunderstand me. I love our honeymoon. I am delighted to be here. I didn't think so at the time, but you could not have brought me anywhere more perfect. We're like Adam and Eve in the primeval garden. If it weren't so cold, I'd walk about naked,' she giggled.

Then she became serious again.

'But all that business about the church . . . as you know I've never been enthusiastic. The bishop was charming. We had a lovely wedding. But it was brought home to me. There should be no doubt about it. I am married to you. I have not the slightest intention of being married to the church. I'm a woman who happens to have fallen in love with a curate. It's not his fault. It's certainly not my fault. Nor should either of us take the blame for it.'

She was, of course, right, sustaining the impasse between us.

CHAPTER 31

But what went ye out into the wilderness for to see?

The sun was warming as we arrived at the gaunt grey house borrowed by Father Tom from the Presbyterians. I was annoyed at the sight of it. As at Llanrhaeadr ym Mochnant, it was another example of classic Victoriana, at odds in every way with the island's primitive character. The grounds outside were uneven, projecting an air of dereliction, suggesting that at one time there had been a garden. Annoyingly, Father Tom's pilgrims had left sacks of rubbish at the back.

'Look at that,' Ann said. She gave them a glare. 'Did they expect somebody to come along with a bin lorry?'

But Guto was right. The house would suit our purposes. The back door was not locked. Our footsteps echoed and re-echoed as we passed through the voluminous empty rooms. We wandered around, chose one we could use as our bedroom, dumped our belongings and returned to the open air. As we left, I picked up my copy of Giraldus.[109]

109 Giraldus Cambrensis, *The Itinerary Through Wales*, 1191, *The description of Wales*, 1194, tr William Llewelyn Williams, 1908

'History is writ large here,' I said as we walked through the Celtic graveyard. 'The Welsh always hated changes imposed on them from the outside. That was their objection to Augustine.'

Ann was surprised.

'I thought they disagreed about the date of Easter.'

I wondered how she knew that. I nodded.

'But Augustine was instituting the authority of Rome. That was the point. And it was still the point in the twelfth century when Gerald of Wales journeyed through this country with Baldwin, the Archbishop of Canterbury. Baldwin celebrated the mass in all four cathedrals. It was his way of establishing his authority over the Welsh. He had a cheek.' I grinned. 'Why is Trefaldwyn the Welsh for Montgomery? It means 'Baldwin's town'. Some little sycophant was sucking up to the archbishop. So, what else did he find?'

I fished out an extract from Geraldus to show her:

> *Beyond Lleyn, there is a small island inhabited by very religious monks, called Caelibes, or Colidei. This island, either from the wholesomeness of its climate, or owing to its vicinity to Ireland, or rather from some miracle obtained by the merits of the saints, has this wonderful peculiarity, that the oldest people die first, because diseases are uncommon and scarcely any die except from extreme old age. Its name is Enlli in the Welsh, and Bardsey in the Saxon language; and very many bodies of saints are*

said to be buried here, and amongst them Daniel, bishop of Bangor. [110]

'He also discovered something else. The monks remained independent, retaining the Celtic spirit, not linked to any order . . . though it was not to last long after that.' I pointed at the remains of the monastery. 'An abbey was founded here in the year 1212 in the name of the Austin Canons Regular.'

We were hungry. We returned to the house for the meal supplied by the hotel. There were cold meats, salad and pickles, bread and butter pudding and a bottle of Chateauneuf-du-Pape. As might be expected, the food was excellent.

'Nor will you be surprised,' I said as we returned to the open air, 'to hear that the next interference came from King Henry VIII. The abbey was dissolved by the king's commissioners in 1537, valued at forty-six pounds, one shilling and four pence halfpenny. You would have thought it hardly worth their while. But it meant, as with Baldwin, that the English church was as much imposed here as it was in

110 *'Jacet autem extra Lhein insula modica quam monachi inhabitant religiosissimi, quos Coelibes vel Colideos vocant. Haec autem insula, vel ab aeris salubritate quam ex Hiberniae confinio sortitur, vel potuis aliquo ex miraculo et sanctorum meritis, hoc mirandum habet, quod in ea seniors praemoriuntur, quia morbi in ea rarissima; et raro vel nunquam hic quisquam moritur, nisi longa senectute confectus. Haec insula Enthli Kambrice vocatur, et longua Saxonica Bardeseie. Et inea, ut fertur, infinita sanctorum sepulta sunt corpora; ibique jacere testantur corpus beati Danielis Banchhorensis escopi.'*

London or York. The people of Wales wanted nothing to do with it.' I turned and pointed out the chapel. 'So, the Welsh went in the opposite direction, given to the '*hwyl*',[111] hymn singing and rampant revivalism.'

'I want to see inside,' she said.

The pitch pine door to the entrance was locked, more resistant than the house to intruders, but we found the key under a stone. It was immediately evident that, with the exception of Father Tom's masses, the building had not been used for years. In the vestry we found a damp register from the 1910s, the services presided over by 'Y Parchedig[112] Moses R Moses, MA Oxon'.

'Fancy,' I said, 'being a student at Oxford only to end up here.'

'I can't but feel sorry for the poor man, particularly since he was saddled with a name like that.' A gleam appeared in her eye. 'Your surname is Moses, so what are you going to call the baby? Moses!'

'It's something of a Welsh custom,' I replied, 'as in the case of the hymnologist William Williams.'

The chapel was remarkable, nevertheless. For all the years of neglect, the interior remained in good condition, complete with a formidable '*set fawr*'.[113] Ann climbed up to take a preacher's eye view.

'Are you going to deliver a sermon?' I laughed.

111 fervent preaching

112 translated as 'the reverend'

113 deacon's pew

She was always wonderful to look at. There was an awkward fragility to her, femininity personified, elegant, intrinsically English, quite at odds with what I envisaged of the Reverend Moses R. Moses that once stood there. Her message was no less uncompromising.

'My darling Richard,' she said, 'is a minister of the Church in Wales, which makes not the slightest sense in the modern world. Look at this building. It's a relic of the superstitious past. Religion is dead. We should not we regret it, the source of so much misery in the history of the world. The only ones who make sense are outright atheists like me, people that refuse to believe in any such nonsense.'

I was reminded of Nancy who could be no less forthright. Ann looked at me naughtily.

'But if Richard insists on his ridiculous superstitions, why, oh why does he fall for such an impossibly inappropriate woman like me?' She grinned down at me. 'Or does he relish being seduced by a randy, hot-blooded infidel?'

She had pinpointed my confusion of mind. I loved her. Nobody else in the world would do. But I remained committed to my faith.

CHAPTER 32

. . . a reed shaken with the wind

Guto and Iona came to visit us later . . . which was just as well. We had cereals for breakfast and half a bottle of milk refrigerated in the stream, but the sea air had made us hungry. For all the ample provisions provided for us by the hotel we had eaten all the rest of the food. Fortunately, Guto brought not only fish but cabbage, runner beans, potatoes and a primus paraffin stove. The fish was of a variety I had never seen before, deep green with a clean white underbelly.

'These are pollock,' he said, 'I caught them this morning after you left.'

Nothing could have been more appetising than fish newly taken out of the sea.

'Don't think Enlli is only to do with saints,' he said. 'The English word "Bardsey" commemorates a Viking chief called 'Barda'. Later there were pirates and smugglers on the island. At one time the Knights Templar had a chapel here. But we have always remained independent . . . which is why for many years we had our own king. When old Mister Love Pritchard was King of Bardsey during the

First World War, the British refused to allow him to join the army because he had reached the age of seventy. It annoyed him enormously. He became quite rebellious. So, he turned traitor and swore allegiance to Kaiser Wilhelm II. It's amazing he was not locked in the Tower of London.'

But there was a meal to prepare. I talked to Iona while Ann peeled the potatoes and Guto was gutting the fish. The girl was uncommunicative at first, but gradually she opened up. From what I could make of her, she was an intelligent young woman, not entirely uneducated. There was a primary school on the island when she was a child. But tired of the isolation, many families had moved back the mainland.

'That's why there are so many empty houses,'[114] she said.

The school, it transpired, was closed in 1953 when she was twelve.

'My father tried to teach me after that. But every time, very quickly, he became incredibly cross.'[115]

Again, I detected the wild streak in her. She far too overtly interested in the opposite sex. What could become of her? It was difficult to envisage. Apart from anything else, how would she manage when she didn't speak English?

'We will leave you to it,' Guto said as they left. 'My wife Elen will have made us a meal.'

114 *'Dyna pam y mae ne gymaint o dai gwag.'*

115 *'Ceisiodd fy nhad fy nysgu at ol hynny. Ond ar ol ychyig roedd pob amser wedi digio yn anfeidrol.'*

We had brought two sleeping bags, but Ann insisted we should fit ourselves into one. I had not suspected it. Perhaps she was more nervous than I thought. In the event it wasn't feasible.

We made a bed with hay from the barn, using the sleeping bags as covers under which we clung together. It was an amorous if not an entirely comfortable night. In the morning it was still dark, the atmosphere eerie, the wind outside whipping up the trees. We ate the remaining cornflakes, packed our belongings and found a spade to bury the rubbish, most of it discarded by the disciples of Father Tom.

'I hate doing this,' she said. 'Waste should be recycled, but what else can we do?'

We trekked back the way we came. Guto was there when we arrived, his boat dipping and rising on the swell. We went over the rocks and cambered aboard. We had, I realised, learned a great deal . . . not so much about the island as about ourselves.

The sea was not particularly wild as we set out, the wind skimming the tips of the waves. East of the bird sanctuary the weather took a distinct turn for the worse. Guto seemed unperturbed. All he did was work the tiller. The leak to the petrol tank was evidently repaired. Then the seas began to mount, rising incrementally from one moment to the next, the propeller fizzing angrily as the stern bucked momentarily out of the water. Already it was terrifying. We could easily be capsized and that would be end of us. To avoid being caught amidships, Guto pointed the boat directly at the waves. It required some dexterity . . . such was the capricious nature of the seas. But there was a certain equilibrium to it. Perhaps it explained the central positioning of the motor.

The surges continued to increase. Soon they appeared like the sides of mountains rising precipitously out of the deep, the propeller like a whirling dervish as we were thrown upwards then brought crashing down into the trough. Ann was shivering like a leaf. Then it began to rain, the wind lashing into my face so I could hardly make out Guto at the helm. I closed my eyes. I prayed for him and for ourselves. And then I prayed again. Ann clung to me. I felt incredibly responsible. At the apex of a wave, I looked over at the headland. I could imagine it, serene as ever on an everyday Tuesday morning, normal and unperturbed, if only we could ever get that far. My soul was intensively given to prayer, promising I would never go to sea again should we, as hardly seemed possible, survive the present ordeal, Guto, my beloved Ann and me. An irrelevant thought struck me. I had always objected to prayer under duress, but I was doing it now. I postponed the idea to be thought about later.

And so, we arrived on the beach at Aberdaron. I looked at my watch. It was half past seven. We had been at sea about an hour. The weather was not particularly hostile as before.

'It was a bit of a go,' Guto laughed. 'I've seen a great deal worse. I hope you weren't too uncomfortable.'

CHAPTER 33

But what went ye out for to see?

It took no more than ten minutes before we crashed out on the bed. We slept huddled together . . . I have no idea for how long before I woke with a start. My back ached. I looked at my watch. It was eight thirty. Breakfast was being served in the dining room of the hotel. It seemed so ordinary after the ordeal of the waves. I eased myself off the bed. Ann was asleep. There seemed no reason to wake her. I peeled off my anorak and stripped to the waist before resorting to a washbasin in the corner.

'What are you doing?' Ann said.

I dried my face and went over to give her a kiss.

'I would have thought it was obvious.'

'I mean, what are we going to do now?'

'Get changed and have breakfast.'

She too had recovered her composure.

'I suppose you're right . . . but not yet. I will begin by having a shower.'

She scrambled off the bed, grabbed her dressing gown and disappeared into the corridor.

Breakfasts were never less than leisurely at the hotel, civilised, with coffee and croissants, tomatoes, eggs, sausages and bacon. We were asked repeatedly, 'How was your trip?'

The manager was more perceptive.

'Did you find what you were looking for on the island?' he asked.

'I don't know,' I replied. 'It remains to be seen. I will have to think about it.'

'I didn't like the thought of it,' Ann said. 'But when I got there, I positively loved it . . . that is until this morning when we might have been drowned. I wondered whether we would survive.'

He was unsurprised.

'That's why the saints chose Enlli. The weather in the sound is often adverse.'

It seemed to me an understatement. But there was no doubt about it . . . we had skirted the fringes of the Celtic world.

Later that afternoon, we took the car on the pilgrimage route as far as the parish of Llangwnadl, the penultimate staging post some six miles north of Aberdaron. I knew nothing about the church. Fortunately, there was a guidebook on sale. The settlement was founded in the sixth century by Saint Gwynhoedl, another of the Celtic saints, who also had links with Welsh folklore. According to the legend of 'Cantre's Gwaelod' his father, Seithennyn, was responsible for the flooding of Cardigan Bay.[116]

'There's something all too human about these myths,' I said. 'As in the story of Cain and Abel people believed what they wanted to believe. What we hear of St Gwynhoedl's father reinforces the point. The story is quite haunting, but why did they say he got drunk and flooded Cardigan Bay? They cherished the thought of a mythical long-lost terrain. Somewhere in their hearts they believed it.'

116 According to *The Black Book of Carmarthen*, 'Cantre's Gwaelod' was a legendary land that subsisted below sea level, protected by seawalls. It was lost when an inebriated Seithennyn forgot to close the sluices.

CHAPTER 34

The quick and the dead

Predictably, there were changes on our return.

'I shall miss our little rendezvous on a Sunday morning,' said Miss Elizabeth Jones, 'but you have a wife to look after you now.'

I was not at all sure about that. Ann was not exactly house-wifely.

'Now you're married, I don't suppose we will see so much of you,' Roger Parker said when we were invited to coffee. He laid on the charm. It was the first time he had held an intimate conversation with Ann. 'Your husband has been very kind to us. I hope he will sometimes be able to take us out in the car.'

It was quite moving, the first time I had been called her husband.

'We will not neglect you,' I promised, 'I know how much it means.'

It was an exciting time for further developments, adding new and different perspectives to my curacy. But on one point I was certain ... there was no denying the elation of our love life.

Ann bought a copy of the *Times Educational Supplement* and began to apply for teaching posts, hoping for an appointment to a secondary school for the beginning of the autumn term. Since she had time of her hands, she also borrowed a selection of Ronnie's sample wallpapers and paint charts with the intention of redecorating the flat. On most evenings we went out for drinks with Ronnie and Val, which was one aspect of life I found particularly satisfactory.

As she had agreed, while Ann was married to me, she was not married to the church. But she saw no reason to make an issue of it, so she attended the services at St Mary's from time to time while keeping her convictions, or rather the absence of them, to herself. Not only that, but people evidently liked her. She fitted in a great deal better than I thought.

It was quite striking. The vicar had a group of supporters around him, what Miss Elizabeth Jones called 'his cronies', the parish treasurer, the churchwardens and the members of the Parochial Church Council, or the PCC. But there was no such structure surrounding the curate. Nor were there any particular rules as to what he should do.

It was illustrated almost immediately on my return. Having pondered the antecedents of one burial ground, I was immediately confronted with another. The churchyard at St Mary's was to be cleared of gravestones. It was finally decided. The PCC had passed it unanimously. The brigadier was away at a regimental dinner. Why had it not been done before? The law had been changed.[117] By Victorian legislation[118] a grave

117 *Town and Country Planning (Churches, Places of Religious Worship and Burial Grounds) Regulations 1950*

118 *Burial Acts,* 1852–85

was to be preserved indefinitely. If ever there was a legislative absurdity, that was it. Even the sun will not last for ever. The predicament would have been even greater had the law been in place earlier. The vicar was quite funny about it. He cited the First Gravedigger in *Hamlet* (*'Alas poor Yorick! I knew him, Horatio, a man of infinite jest'*),[119] after which he threw the skull away and carried on digging. The recycling of graves was commonplace in Shakespeare's day.

There remained, nevertheless, a series of regulations to which the PCC must comply. Over a hundred years had passed since the burial ground at St Mary's was declared closed. The parish could therefore apply for a faculty[120] which gave rise to further bureaucracy. The plan had to be publicised in the parish magazine and in the local newspapers. The procedure raised no great difficulty, but it took an inordinate amount of time. By a rear-guard action of the brigadier, a number of people tried to make a fuss. Their objections were not unsurmountable. Nor were we approached by any surviving relatives. When the faculty was granted, we proceeded.

The contractors were to start work on Ascension Day, 7th May, at which point I was expected to play my part. The vicar's instructions were specific. I was to make a full and detailed plan of the churchyard before the evidence was

119 *Hamlet*, Act 5, Sc 1

120 The issue of a faculty allows the church authorities to evade the jurisdiction of Town and Country Planning.

taken away . . . which meant making a record of each gravestone, its position and inscription. It was a daunting responsibility. It was never once mentioned. For so precise and exhaustive an undertaking the parish should have engaged a chartered surveyor, such as those in the employ of Neville Bithell at Bingham Price . . . whose services were readily to hand. But that would have cost the parish money, so for that reason, it was delegated to the curate.

It seemed to me an affront. I took it up with the vicar. Were there not more important things for his curate to do? To that he was unforthcoming. As usual, there was nothing I could do about it, so, I equipped myself with a clipboard and spent a couple of hours the evening before in the lower section of the graveyard. It was easier said than done as I made a record of the positions and, insofar as they were legible, inscriptions on the memorial of each grave. In places, the stones were broken, or the lettering had simply crumpled away, and since the installation of memorial stones was not obligatory, I could not record the contents of unmarked graves. The task was slow and arduous. Then, on the following morning, after the vicar and I had read the Daily Office, I approached the low loader that appeared on the High Street below.

The driver extended a cheerful hand out of the door of the cab.

'Morning, reverend. I'm Charlie.' He nodded in the direction of the unseen accomplice sitting beside him. 'And this is Jimmy'.

He opened the driver's door, swivelled himself round and jumped out, a short, plumpish man, probably in his late forties, with a scrawny residue of red hair. Jimmy, when he appeared, was taller, thin and, I thought, rather morose. With them was a chunky lad called Pete. Charlie looked up at the church then nodded at the large yellow caterpillar tractor parked on the deck behind.

'Begging your pardon, reverend, but how the hell am I going to get that all the way up there?'

I could see what he meant . . . though in the event it was nothing like so difficult as it appeared. Pete took up a wheelbarrow loaded with spades, hammers, pickaxes and much else. Then Jimmy went to work removing a section of the railings while Charlie chugged the machine up the steep side of the mound.

And that was where the problems began. The caterpillar tractor was some twenty feet long with a cabin for the driver and a wide shovel scoop at the front. The first set of stones had to be removed by hand. There was no room between the gravestones to allow the machine onto the site. But what surprised me were the objections of the men.

'I don't like it, reverend,' Jimmy said. 'I really don't like it at all. It's not right to mess around when people have passed away.'

Charlie seemed no less disturbed. He may have been a big, burly man, but he gave a positive shiver.

'Now that I see the job in front of me,' he said, peering through the windscreen of the cab, 'I don't want to do it. I'd rather not do it at all, thank you very much.' He climbed out. 'I think I'll ring the boss.'

The boy Pete said nothing, but he evidently shared their feelings. I did my best to reassure them, reiterating what I usually said whenever I was arranging a funeral.

'The souls of the dead are long gone,' I said. 'All we have here is the reverent disposal of human remains.'

The discussion went on for some time. Finally, reluctantly, they agreed. The first headstones did not seem particularly large, but I was astonished to discover just how heavy they were.

Progress was made over the next few days. It was hard to keep up. I found myself working overtime. It was incredible how quickly an area could be cleared. The displaced stones were piled up in heaps. There had been some discussion about them at the PCC. A number of the flat headstones could be used to pave footpaths, but there were far more of them available than would be needed for that. There were ethical issues at stake, too. They may have been decayed and decrepit, but these were crafted works of masonry, dedicated and paid for by the relatives of the deceased . . . not unlike, if not so profligate, as Anne Davies' commitment to the 'man with the egg'. A local builder would give money for the stone, but they could not possibly be sold. It was finally decided. The surplus memorials would have to be retained within the churchyard. A pit was to be excavated where they could be interred. I wondered what they did with redundant gravestones in Shakespeare's day.

There was a further point to it. The churchyard should retain its epitaphic character. Notable or singular memorials should be kept. Of particular importance, Richard Wilson, the pioneer of English landscape painting,[121] is buried near the clergy vestry on the north side. His tombstone was to be left untouched. There were also others, I discovered, of peculiar interest. One from the 1870s had accommodated ten separate burials, allowing for the deceased of both sexes to be interred within the one grave. It was not difficult to explain. St Mary's stands on a prehistoric man-made mound, allowing for burials at almost any depth. At the base of the inscription that bore their names were the words, 'Daniel Jones, owner'. I wondered how he got away with it.[122] Perhaps he made an unsavoury arrangement with the vicar of the day. There were also many examples of graveyard doggerel:

When I am dead and in my grave,
I pray the Lord my soul will save . . .

Those too I decided to keep.

I continued to compile my records every evening after the men had finished work, anticipating their progress the following day. There were always new problems and developments. It was never less than fascinating. The land was

121 1714–82

122 Burials in churchyards are free. A charge is made for the maintenance of the graves.

churned up. There were great mounds of earth everywhere. A considerable number of gravestones had been removed, piled up ready for their further disposal. Then, one day when I went up, the caterpillar tractor was standing idly by while the two men and the boy were sitting on the entrance steps to the church. When he saw me, Charlie leaped up.

'Reverend, reverend, so glad you did come.'

It took but a moment to explain. Some of the memorials were large and elaborate so that, from their external appearance, there was no way of knowing whether they stood over a grave or a funerary vault. The machine had knocked the top off a vault. They were at a loss as to what to do about it. I went to take a look.

I too was not impervious to it. It was as though the deceased had been betrayed, the point accentuated by the white marble plinth bearing a broken-winged fallen angel lying on its side. There was a plaque telling me that this was the ancestral burial place of a family called Jones of Colomendy Hall.[123] The earliest interment was dated 20th June 1719. Then, not knowing quite what to expect, I climbed over a mound of earth to inspect the vault itself. What I saw was breath-taking . . . a brick-lined aperture containing a series of stone plinths of different sizes, each sustaining a decorative burial casket made of lead, individually designed, ornate, bearing what could not but be a silver plate so tarnished it was black. I had never seen,

123 Richard Wilson died at Colomendy on 15th May,1782. He was a cousin of the owner, Catherine Jones, 1701–86.

nor ever anticipated seeing anything remotely like this, nothing more indicative of wealth and privilege, even in death a world set apart. They pre-dated the Victorian legislation, but they represented precisely the same sentiment, anticipating that their mortal remains be left untouched for the rest of eternity.

I knew it was ridiculous; nevertheless, I found the thought disturbing, as though I were an intruder into a world apart, like some latter-day Howard Carter confronted with the long-lost tomb of Tutankhamun. (I could not bring myself to believe in the curse.) Still, the thought was haunting. I wondered how they went about interring the saints in that bleak, unkempt burial ground on Bardsey. Since there were supposedly twenty thousand of them, the graves must have been recycled and recycled again. As I had explained to the men, there need not be a fuss. Burial is the reverent disposal of human remains. I talked to Ann about it afterwards.

'What brought me back to reality were the lead caskets. They must be worth a mint,' I said.

She was intrigued.

'So, what did you do?'

'What else could I do? Their final resting place was violated. I buried them as before,' I said, but I had mixed feelings about it.

CHAPTER 35

The ordination

Nothing could have been more important than my ordination to the priesthood on Trinity Sunday, 24th May. I left our marital bed with regret to take part in the pre-ordination retreat. The arrangements were as before. The candidates were given accommodation in the bleak, dispiriting rooms of the Gladstone Library. When we were not being lectured on the joys of the spiritual life, we were expected to maintain protracted periods of silence, meditation and prayer. For all my terror of the waves off the coast of Aberdaron, I was no better at it than I was before.

I did find something to distract me. The Reverend Maldwyn Dwyfor Jones was staying at the library, a fledgling minister of the Calvinistic Methodists. I had known him a little during our student days at Bangor. He was brimming with enthusiasm.

'We should get back to the Bible,' he said, 'the wonderful word of God. Perhaps we could organise a Billy Graham crusade. We can't get the great man himself, but we can find ways to follow in his footsteps.'

It was not his fault that I found him infuriating. I decided to provoke him.

'Did you know that King Solomon was an aficionado of oral sex?'

He looked horrified.

'How dare you say that? No reference could possibly be made to any such thing in the pages of the holy scripture.'

I pointed out the reference in *The Authorised Version*: 'Thy navel is like a round goblet which wanteth not liquor.'[124]

He went to find *Y Beibl Cyssegr Lân.*[125] There was a look of triumph in his face.

'William Morgan did not mistranslate the holy scriptures. Undoubtedly, it is about the lady's navel.'

'That's where you're mistaken,' I replied. 'There can be no such thing as a tumescent navel.'

At the time I thought it funny . . . though afterwards I was rather ashamed of it.

The pre-ordination retreat came and went. The service, I knew, would be no less protracted than it was before. We spilled out into the cathedral yard when Mattins was done, allowing us to greet our families, friends and other such well-wishers as had made a point of turning up. The sun was shining. It was a lovely day. There was no small amount of chatter as Ann arrived, her skirt all but around her waist as she straddled the pillion of a miniscule BSA Bantam[126]

124 Song of Solomon 7, 2a

125 *'Dy fogail fydd fel gorflwch crwn , heb eifiau lleithder . . .'*

126 A two-stroke motorcycle produced by the Birmingham Small Arms Company, 1948–71.

ridden by Sophie Mortmain, a larger than average bishop's daughter we had known at university. Ann and I hardly had time to speak before we were expected back in the cathedral for the ceremony to begin.

So, we proceeded. I had been less attentive to the details when I was ordained to the deaconate. Now I took notice. When it came to the promises, there is no doubting the prevarication that is liturgically built in:

> *Bishop: Will you be diligent to frame and fashion your own selves, and your families, according to the Doctrine of Christ, and to make both yourselves and them, as much as in you lieth, wholesome examples and patterns to the flock of Christ?*
>
> *Answer: I will apply myself thereto, the Lord being my helper.*

There was no avoiding the 'as much as in you lieth' acknowledgement of human fallibility. But there was the other point. Ann was quite impossible to 'frame and fashion', not that I was going to admit it to anyone. But I had got used to the idea as I would not have it otherwise. I may have profoundly disagreed with her, but under all and any circumstances, I was prepared to exonerate her disbeliefs.

Then came the moment of the ordination itself, fulfilling my vocation. The assembled clergy gathered round as we knelt before them, each reaching out to share with the bishop in the laying on of hands:

> *Receive the Holy Ghost for the Office and Work of a Priest in the Church of God, now committed unto thee by the imposition of our hands. Whose sins thou dost forgive, they are forgiven; and whose sins thou dost retain they are retained.*

For all my reservations, I found it deeply moving, allowing for the cure of souls, the absolution of the sins of the world. What did Jesus say to the woman caught in the act of adultery?

> *. . . hath no man condemned thee? She said, No man, Lord. And Jesus said unto her, Neither do I condemn thee: go and sin no more*[127*]

It emancipated her. But under what circumstances would I want to retain a person's sins? I did not know the answer to that. There was one consolation. My priesthood perpetuated Christ's heritage at the Last Supper, dispensing the salvation of mankind through the bread and the wine of eternal life.

I had always found one aspect moving, the point reinforced when I celebrated the Holy Communion at St Mary's the following week. I was fascinated by the hands of the people receiving Communion. I had noticed them when dispensing the chalice. When I gave them the bread,

127 John 8, 10b–11

their hands were even more in evidence . . . a labourer's hands gnarled and cut about, teenage hands not yet entirely touched by human affairs, a housewife's hands marked and scored in the course of her husbandry. No wonder I was ordained by the imposition of hands.

CHAPTER 35

Life's young dream

It was a time for new beginnings, the point underpinned when I received a letter from my brother-in-law. He was to give me his car. Roger let me borrow the Snipe from time to time, but it was no substitute for my having a vehicle of my own. Now, I was being given a car. It may have been twenty-seven years old, but from what I envisaged of it, it was a wonderful, sensationally vintage MG called Bluebell. It had been the car of my sister Jean's husband, Les. By dint of their generosity, it was to be mine. I could hardly wait.

Ann and I took a bus into Chester. They lived in a semi-detached house near Alexandra Park.

'I'm not sure I should let you have it,' Les said. 'But the firm is allowing me a vehicle for my work, which means I've nowhere to put it. And don't get too excited. It's not exactly in the best of condition.' He pulled a face. 'I don't think either of us can afford to do it up. But it might keep you going for a while.'

I had always felt rather sorry for Les. I loved his quirky Liverpudlian humour and his upbeat scouser twang. He should have been a farmer. In his heart it was what he had always wanted. But he was brought up in Huyton, a sprawling Liverpool suburb, which meant he had no real connections with the farming world. So, having been to Agricultural College followed by a degree reading Botany at Bangor University, during which time he met Jean, the best he could do was to take up a job as an agricultural consultant and sales manager. It seemed he was well paid, but it was hardly the answer to life's young dream.

On the other hand, I could not have been more enthusiastic about the car. I had never seen it, though during the previous week I had found photographs of a two-seater MG Midget from the 1930s, which meant I knew more or less what to expect. It sounded an absolute treasure, of the same vintage as the MG Magnette that won the Mille Miglia[128] of its class in 1933. When we went out onto a back street to see it, I was not disappointed. As expected, it was bright blue with a canvas hood, while the coachwork seemed rather less battered than I had been led to believe. Indubitably, calculatedly, the car was made for speed, with great circular headlamps, a stretched-out bonnet and the sweeping curved fenders over its multi-spoked wheels. Never was there a better example of get up and go. Most of the vehicle was taken up by the engine compartment, a classic racing machine with the driver at its tail. I got in. My legs were extended out a full stretch before I could reach the pedals. I could only just see over the bonnet.

We spent some time after lunch going through the paperwork. Les had filled in and posted the section that

128 a thousand-mile round trip race between Rome and Brescia

transferred the car to me. I had taken out a third-party, fire and theft insurance with the Ecclesiastical Insurance Company, which was all I could afford. He gave me the registration document which I was to sign and send off. That done, we discussed the vehicle's technicalities. What he told me was quite mysterious. I hardly understood a word of it. Unlike the Ford Populars which were furnished with a flathead system where the poppet valves were contained within the cylinder block, the MG possessed an overhead valve engine with the cylinder head above the combustion chamber. Unlike more recent vehicles, the accelerator pedal was positioned between the pedals for the break and the clutch. Apparently, this was usual in vehicles of that age, but I found it alarming. I was likely to run into the car in front.

Having thanked them both again, Les adjusted the canvas over our heads and we set off. It was raining as we left. The car, I discovered, was possessed of one further peculiarity . . . we were overtaken incessantly. It would only go thirty miles an hour, downhill with the wind behind it. Finally, just after midnight, we arrived back in Mold. I had arranged with the vicar for the MG to be parked in a corner of the drive outside the vicarage. He had agreed to it, rather grudgingly.

'I don't want it stationed there permanently,' he said. 'It would be very unsightly.'

A point with which I could not but disagree. It had been a grand house in its day, but nothing could disguise the dreary environs of the present.

Into the small hours over a not so abstemious number of glasses of wine, we discussed the problems that surrounded the MG. Ann was unconvinced.

'Let's see if we can give it a bit more go,' she said.

The following morning, I drove down to Pete Williamson's garage in New Street. He was known as a bit of a rogue, but I liked him.

'This car,' he pronounced definitively, having taken no more than a cursory look, 'should not be on the road. I wouldn't drive it to the end of our street. Vehicles like that are a danger to the public.' He looked me in the eye. 'Let me give you some advice, reverend. No, I'll do better than that. I'll send it to the knackers myself. If you want a proper car, you should come to me. I'll be happy to fit you up.'

I thought, he would say that, so I decided to carry on using it.

But trundling the MG laboriously up the hill to New Brighton the following Sunday morning was nothing less than a nightmare, though the incline was not particularly steep. I was glad I had not offered the organist a lift. Then it came under the scrutiny of Ginny Bunting, the little old lady in the black sequined hat that rang the bell, reminiscent of the terrible 'Grandma' in the Giles cartoons. She did not feel in the least constrained.

'Where the shit did you find that? It should have been put out for scrap.'

The rest of the New Brightonites when they arrived were no less uncomplimentary. They were not out to be unkind. They simply couldn't help it. That, it transpired, was but the beginning of my woes. Disaster struck at the end of the service. The engine started promptly enough, but no matter into what gear it was put into, the torque was simply not prepared to engage the wheels.

'It's not going to go,' said Fred, the churchwarden, gratuitously.

They all seemed to find it funny. The issue was resolved by Frank.

'Your crown wheel and pinion are bust,' he said.

'It's time to give up wishful thinking,' Ann said, after the organist and I had made our way regretfully down the hill. 'It's a beaten-up old banger and that is all that can to be said about it.'

The very idea I found outrageous. This was no plain car. This was my unique, cherishable, potentially race-winning vintage MG. But as she went on about it, I saw no point in arguing with her. She either recognised the vehicle's merits or she didn't.[129] We spent the rest of the day talking about something else. Nor did I mention it during my meeting with the vicar the following day. He must have noticed it was missing, but he said nothing about it.

But there was no way I was prepared to admit defeat. Pete Williamson would be much too pleased. That evening we went round to Ronnie and Val's. The word had evidently got round.

'People say it's a mobile wreck,' Val said.

129 It's difficult to explain its magic. The letters 'MG' indicate simply 'Morris Garage'.

Ronnie was more constructive.

'Benny, one of my lads, knows a bit about cars. I'll send him round tomorrow evening after work.'

'It's time it was sorted out,' Ann said. 'Richard is like a lost soul.'

I spent the following day having high hopes of Benny. He turned up outside my flat at about half past six in an almost equally decrepit Austin Seven. With him was Doug, another of Ronnie's employees.

'Let's see if we can make sense of it, reverend,' he said. 'We'll go up to New Brighton to take a look.'

Ann, by then, was more conciliatory. She blew me a kiss as we set off. Benny and Doug hardly inspired confidence in their paint-covered overall, yet they made short work of it when we came to the MG. They had a tow rope. They manhandled the car out onto the road and hooked it up.

'You get in and steer, reverend,' Benny said. 'And remember, when I stop, you stop.'

The drive that followed was terrifying. It's a wonder we didn't collide.

'You were riding the brake the whole time,' he said accusingly when we finally arrived outside the vicarage.

What was to happen next? It was difficult to decide. They chocked the vehicle up and poked around underneath.

'It's going to cost at least forty pounds,' Benny said, 'and probably a bit more.'

He left me to think about it. I knew it wasn't feasible. When I told the vicar about it, he was pleased.

'Since your vehicle is not viable,' he said, 'I trust you will dispose of it forthwith.'

As ever, I found him difficult to understand. Nobody could have been more instructive when it came to the whys and wherefores of the faith. Yet in other matters he was unforthcoming. Only Linda was able to treat him with ease. I discussed the car with Les over the phone.

'I'm sorry,' he said. 'I didn't think it would crack up so soon. If it will help, I might be able to spare you a little cash. But things are tight at the start of a new job.'

It was Ronnie that came up with the solution.

'I've seen an old Morris down at the tip,' he said. 'If we can get out the crown wheel and pinion, it will probably fit.'

In some trepidation, I went to see the manager at the National Provincial Bank on the High Street.

'You can afford to spend no more than twenty pounds,' he said. 'The bank will agree to that.'

So, every evening, brooking the vicar's disapproval, what appeared to be a major work of engineering commenced operations outside the vicarage. The MG was cranked up, the chassis propped up on bricks. Benny was the prime mover, assisted by Doug. The wheels and the back axle were removed. The particulars were beyond me, but they seemed to know what they were doing.

Finally, at the end of the week, the car was re-assembled and ready to go. Ronnie and Val came to witness it. Even the vicar and Linda came out.

'Get in, reverend,' Benny said. 'Let's see if it's OK.'

So, I did. The engine revved dutifully as before. I pushed in the clutch and engaged first gear. The car moved backwards! I tried to reverse. The car went forwards! So, that was it. I had four backwards gears and one forwards! Apart from Fred and Benny, everybody found it hilarious. For me it was the end of the line. I had completely run out of money.

Ann and I again discussed it at length. I spoke about it to Les. Then, to my eternal, infinite regret, a vindicated Pete Williamson came with a truck to take the car away. *Requiescat in pace, MG.*

CHAPTER 37

Alarms and excursions

Earlier in the year Roger had asked me if we could visit the International Musical Eisteddfod at Llangollen in the second week of July. It seemed a good idea particularly as, on the Thursday in conjunction with the festival, a full Choral Eucharist was to be celebrated among the nearby ruins of Vale Crucis Abbey.[130*] It was an occasion I knew well. Few services could be more theatrical, intensified by the massed choir of unaccompanied clergy voices as they soar among the bare arches and clerestories.

'I have been asked to arrange the music,' the vicar said when I told him about it. 'By all means bring Dr Parker, but I expect you to sing in the choir. Don't forget to bring your robes.'

We decided to leave early, intending to be there for about ten. The service was to begin at eleven. Roger wanted to

130 Guto'r Glyn, 1412–93, an eminent Welsh poet, was given lodgings at Vale Crucis. On one occasion, wishing to see him usefully employed, the Abbot asked him to take a flock of sheep for sale at the market in Shrewsbury. On his arrival most of the sheep were lost. But he had written several excellent poems.

see the ruins. The journey, I thought, would take the best part of an hour, the most spectacular part of it being the old turnpike road, meandering and clinging to the barren mountainsides as it runs down through the Horseshoe Pass towards Llangollen. At one point I pulled into a layby so that we could admire the view. The road levelled out as we approached the remains of the abbey. I could see the ruins on lower ground a little away to our left. But it was a mistake . . . I had passed the entrance, a rough track forking down from the road. I drove on. There was bound to be another way in, I thought.

There was. But if the earlier angle in had been obtuse, this was no less acute. I pulled the car over to the right then turned the wheel sharply to the left. We edged forwards. It was a disaster. The car descended into the adjoining track with a crunch. I got out. The Snipe was stuck. It would take a crane to move it. All four wheels were off the ground. The back bumper was caught on the edge of the tarmac. The front was wedged solidly on the bank opposite, placing us immovably across the entrance. Already a queue was forming away to my left, a venerable string of clerical vehicles. I could see the Archdeacon of Wrexham's Rover and, further down, the bishop's black Vauxhall Cresta. There was no doubting the consequences. The service would have to be cancelled, torpedoed by 'that young curate of Mold'. There was the blast of a whistle.

'All right, you chaps. There's a bit of a problem here. Jump to it.'

A gang of boy scouts appeared as if from nowhere. They bounced the car round onto the track. The clergy choir sang. The bishop celebrated the eucharist.

But there were disasters in the weeks that followed. First, our Danish chair came suddenly apart, broken in two where the seat had met the back. Ann was not surprised.

'It was unstable,' she said, 'like a half-opened book. The stresses were in the wrong place. The craftsmen tried to make allowances for it, but it shouldn't have worked in the first place.'

I contacted the shop. They were prepared to replace it with something more practical. I was sorry, nevertheless. It had been part of our dream.

The second disaster came as a bombshell. I had thought nothing of it when Ann visited the doctors in the surgeries below. Now she had the result she was furious. So that was why she had set about redecorating the flat. She was three months pregnant. Conception must have taken place during our honeymoon. We had taken precautions, but somehow, she was adamant . . . it was solely and entirely my fault.

'I have told you repeatedly,' she said when she finally decided to resume our relationship, 'I'm a career woman. I did not expect ever to have a child. It's put paid to any hope of my getting a teaching post. They won't have me in this condition.' She waved a finger. 'Abortion is illegal,[131] so I'll have the little bugger adopted. Of that, you can be certain.'

131 The medical termination of pregnancy was permitted under the *Abortion Act 1967*.

I felt helpless. The consequences seemed evident.

'The parish will not like it.'

She gave me a glare.

'Can you think of a better solution? I should never have married a parson.'

'We can't make a secret of it,' I said. 'You don't look it at the moment, but sooner or later, your pregnancy will become obvious.'

It did nothing to improve her frame of mind. She went on muttering about it for days. I did not altogether feel guilty at the thought of our having a child. I had not planned for such a thing to happen, but it was not surprising. Our marriage was forever springing surprises.

But a change was happening to Ann in the weeks that followed. Something of her characteristic logic was missing. Her reactions went strangely awry. She became markedly more clingy, more amorous. It seemed to be instinctive, as though mother nature had taken over. I'd remembered what she had said during our honeymoon. I was surprised, nevertheless, when she raised again the question of the Mothers' Union.

'I still don't want to join the organisation,' she said, 'but I am the curate's wife. I should therefore make allowances. I don't want to upset anybody, least of all Linda. I really like her. She's extremely good fun. She knows how to keep the vicar on track.'

I was not sure what she meant by that. But she had a point . . . the curate's wife would be expected to play her part.

A possibility came to mind.

'The Mothers' Union is a national institution,' I said, 'founded by Mary Sumner in the 1870s. But there is such a thing as The Young Wives. They're not anything like so hidebound as the MU, a junior branch without too many responsibilities. If you want to set something up, that's the way to do it. Nor need they necessarily be mothers.'

A gleam appeared in Ann's eye. The idea clicked. She went off to discuss it with Val. From then on the arrangements proceeded apace. Within days there were plans galore. Members appeared as if from nowhere. A couple of them were also pregnant. I had little to do with them. They met in each other's houses. The Young Wives were a venturesome, lively and interesting bunch. When, by some mischance, they were advertised in the parish magazine as 'The Young Widges', they were never thereafter known as anything else.

There were further developments in the weeks that followed. Ann and Linda became firm friends. Perhaps her pregnancy was something to do with it. The vicar and Linda had a large family of their own. Habitually on a Saturday afternoon we were invited to the vicarage for tea. Even more remarkable was my discovery that, also on a Saturday afternoon, the vicar was addicted to the all-in wrestling matches put out by the ITV. He chortled at the bravado and defiant impudence of the villainous Mick McManus and the diminutive Jackie Pallo as they threw their opponents around the ring. No interest, I thought, could have been stranger for a man of the cloth.

CHAPTER 38

Death row

It had become the custom for whoever was responsible for conducting Evensong at St Mary's on a Sunday evening to afterwards accompany the choir as they sang hymns on one of the wards at the cottage hospital. Roger Parker seemed to find it funny.

'I don't think they will do the patients the slightest good,' he said. 'Hymns can be very depressing.'

He waved a hand in the direction of the bookcase. When I found it, he consulted his copy of *Hymns Ancient and Modern*.

'How about "Art thou weary, are thou languid, art thou sore distressed"? That should put a sparkle into their fizz.' Working his way through the pages, he positively snorted. 'What about "Within the churchyard side by side"? It's a real little corker.'

He read out:

They do not hear when the great bell
Is ringing overhead;
They cannot rise and come to church
With us, for they are dead.

'It's Mrs Alexander at her worst,' I replied. 'Not only funereal but quite terrible doggerel.' A serious thought struck me, and I added, 'It's a piece of social history, though, from the days when whole families were wiped out by TB.'

He shrugged his shoulders.

'We're doctors. We're not magicians.'

I reached out for his copy.

'This is the original edition of *Hymns Ancient and Modern.*[132] That hymn was excluded when *A&M* was revised in 1951.'

He nodded.

'By then we had developed a vaccine.'

I shook my head.

'I don't think the editors would have appreciated that.'

But the hymn-singing sessions were a great deal less stressful than my visits to the wards at other times. There were good reasons for it. We had discussed the erstwhile impact of TB. Now, with the incidence of cancer, a further no less frightening affliction had descended on the world. It led me to wonder about my own smoking habits . . . though Father Tom had been adamant. I remembered his words.

'Tobacco is like the glorious sunshine of the summer and the purifying snow of the winter, one of the most gracious and wonderful endowments of Almighty God. It would be churlish to refuse so divine, rich and unexpected a gift of creation.'

Beware of theologians bearing gifts? He was not entirely impervious, though, hence his adoption of menthol

132 1861, hymn number 575 A&M 1861, 595

cigarettes . . . the mere thought of which I found repellent. But to read about its dangers in the newspapers or to discuss it with Father Tom was one thing. To come up against its stark realities was another. There were no effective treatments. The cancer patients clogged up the wards. So, the main hospitals, such as The Maelor in Wrexham, dumped the cancer patients on the cottage hospitals.

Whenever I went hospital visiting, I was confronted with the anteroom of death. It had its implications for the smokers in the youth club. It had its ramifications for me. But that was not my only worry. As an unseasoned deacon at the age of twenty-four, confronted with so many older, anguished and terminally ill patients, I found what to say to them and how to say it all but impossible. Also, there was a deception to it. It was not the practice to tell them they were expected to die. I talked to these people certainly. I passed the time with them. It was a kind of bankruptcy. No amount of theological training, no protracted periods of contemplative prayer, no knowledge of doctrine or insights into the New Testament were of the slightest use. I was scraping the barrel.

'*Accipe curam meam et tuam*,' the bishop said during my ordination. For some reason he resorted to Latin: 'Receive the cure of souls that is both mine and thine.' Confronted with the reality of the cancer wards, I had every reason to believe I could not cure anything at all.

One day I was approached by the matron.

'I don't want to interrupt your good work, Mr Hughes, but I would be grateful if you would have a word with Jenny

Evans. She's in the bed on the right. She's in something of a state. I've given her an injection, but it will need time to take effect.' She pulled a face. 'In the meantime, she's upsetting the other patients.'

I went over and a nurse drew the curtains around us.

'Mrs Jennifer Evans?'

'Miss,' she said.

She was no older than Rosie. But her face was grey, drawn and emaciated, a terrified young woman in the final reaches of her life. I took a chair and sat beside her.

'They don't tell you a thing in this place,' she said. 'But I'm not a fool. It's obvious.' She grabbed my arm in a vice-like grip. 'I've never been religious. I've never felt the need for it. I don't know any prayers. But now there's nothing else for it.' I could see the pain in her eyes. 'Please. I need to pray. I need to pray now.'

I did not even think about it.

'We'll say it together,' I said. '"Our Father . . .".'

Her eyes melted. She had known it all along, the first, fundamental commonplace of the Christian life. Never was there so intense a moment of catharsis. As I came away, I knew I had done nothing, but I had also, I thought, done everything

CHAPTER 39

Betrayal

Again, I met her on the High Street. 'I'm deserted,' Nancy said, 'Peter is away in Nottingham on a course, some do organised by Boots.' She put a persuasive hand on my arm. 'But you know me. Whatever else I'm a social being. I wonder if you and your wife Ann would like to come to tea.' Perhaps I should have been more circumspect. Nancy could be too inquisitive by half. I accepted her invitation nevertheless. It was arranged for the following Wednesday afternoon. 'You know where I live,' she said. I did indeed. It had haunted my conscience ever since, that remarkable amnesic New Year's Eve when the three of us drank far too much.

You really shouldn't have bothered,' Nancy said when Ann presented her with a bunch of flowers. She invited us in and went to find a vase. I had not taken much notice of my surroundings when I was there before. Nancy, I remembered, had described herself as pig ignorant. But there was nothing in the least ignorant about the drawing room which had deep capacious armchairs, fashionable G plan furniture and a series of decorative watercolours hung on the walls. The dining room was no less elegant. Furthermore, Nancy had gone to some trouble. The little savouries and cup cakes were homemade.

She poured out the teas then turned her attention to Ann. 'Richard is forever pontificating at the church,' she said, 'but I have not had the opportunity of meeting you. I gather you're from Liverpool.' Her eyes twinkled 'You could have fooled me. You don't sound in the least like a scouser.' 'I can turn the accent on if you like,' Ann replied. 'She calls policemen "rozzers",' I said. Nancy nodded. 'You met at Bangor University.' 'It's a university college,' I replied, 'part of the University of Wales.' It had always amused me. 'But the city council suffers from delusions of grandeur. A notice on the outskirts calls Bangor "The Athens of Wales".'

Nancy's eyes sparkled. 'So how did you two meet?' How could I possibly forget it? 'I was incredibly lucky,' I said, 'at least I thought so at the time. The new wing had yet to be opened when I was first at Church Hostel. I shared a large ramshackle bedroom with three other students who habitually stayed up until three in the morning. Scenes, you may say, from student life. A vicar's son from Machynlleth was the worst. The cleaners complained that our room was full of cigarette ash. 'No,' he said. 'You can blame the others. I put all mine behind that radiator over there.' Never was there a man more oblivious. He kept a loaf in his locker for so long that, when it was found, a mouse had eaten a corridor right through from one side to the other.'

I smiled. 'And then? I was privileged. Church Hostel stands high on the hillside overlooking the Menai Straights. When the new wing was opened, I was given the best of all the bedrooms, larger than the others, in a little wing by itself with windows that overlooked the scenery. It could not have been more spectacular, with Telford's magnificent suspension bridge tucked away down to the left. It gave me a thrill every morning when I opened the curtains and looked out. I remember walking down there to examine the bridge. But what struck me was the wreck on the shore below of a black and white corvette, HMS Conway, used as a training ship but originally a ship of the line, the saddest of all sights, left to moulder after being wrecked while it was being moved.'

I gave Nancy another smile. 'And then? Nearing the end of the term, it was my twenty-first birthday on 19th December. So, on a bring a bottle basis, I decided to invite twenty-one guests for drinks in my room. I counted them earlier in the day. I had twenty people coming. So I asked a girl called Marie if she could bring a friend. She brought Ann. I had seen her before. She had not noticed me. But she noticed me then. Being a Saturday night there was a dance in the Pritchard Jones Hall at the college. So after the party we did the conga along the road to join in. Ann and I danced, we danced and we danced again. Need I say more?'

The conversation drifted on for some time before Nancy finally went for the jugular. 'What did you make of Father Tom?' Ann reacted instantly. 'He's a drama queen,' she replied. 'I don't know why anybody takes him seriously.' Nancy pulled a face. 'Richard thinks he's brilliant.' Ann nodded. 'I don't like him. He puts on too many airs and graces.' She shrugged her shoulders. 'It doesn't really matter.

Father Tom had been turfed him out. He's no longer chaplain to the college.' Nancy turned accusingly to me. 'I think there's a bit more to it than that. You didn't tell me half of what there is to be said about Father Tom. He wasn't exactly kind to either of you.'

She leant forwards. 'One of my friends organises the catering supplies for the Students' Union at Bangor. She has worked there for years. I asked her if she remembered you and Ann. She did. It was quite the talk of the town. She told me about your little fiasco with Father Tom.' It came as a shock, the last thing I wanted to hear. 'I know it took place some six years ago,' Nancy continued. 'But my friend remembers it well.' Suddenly she became quite concerned. 'I don't want you start worrying about it. I'm not going to spread gossip around the parish. I'm discretion itself. But I do love a good scandal.' She turned her attention to me. 'Why don't you tell me the whole story?'

It seemed I had no choice. 'It started innocuously enough,' I said. 'Why do people fall in love? Ann calls it an imperative of nature.' I looked at Nancy. 'But we've already talked about this. You remember what we said about Elvis? Love is like that. You're all shook up. It's unexpected. It comes at you from nowhere.' I thought a moment. 'There were contributory factors though they're difficult to define. I suppose I was ready for it. I wanted there to be a change in my life.' I looked at Ann. 'But having found each other, there is no way we could let it go. We want to be together to the end of time.'

There was, though, a further point to it. 'You should also,' I said, 'understand my reactions to Father Tom. Ann has no time for him. But as I told you, I had never met so singular or remarkable a priest. My father was stuffy and conservative. Father Tom was the complete opposite . . . liberty unrestrained. I remember walking into his study one day when he was talking on the phone. 'I won't be a moment,' he said. 'I'm having a word with Enid.' It took me a moment to realise that he was talking to Dr Enid Wellington, principal of the Church in Wales Teacher Training college on the other side of the city. I had always thought her a stuffy old bird. 'Now come on, Fanny,' he said. 'What the fuck are you thinking? It's time you stopped wanking about.' 'I can't believe it,' I said when he had finished. 'Do you always talk to her like that?' He gave me a naughty grin. 'She positively loves it.'

'That,' I said, 'was the backdrop to all that followed. Father Tom broke the rules with impunity. Old bats like Enid Wellington were eating out of his hand.' It continued to amaze me when I thought about it. 'You have to understand,' I said. 'I was young and optimistic. So what happened next? Ann was locked out of her lodgings one night when we stayed out late. So I smuggled her into Church Hostel, split my divan bed in two and gave a place to sleep for the night. Did we have sex? Of course not. We were in no position to procreate a child. Nor, I thought, was there anything particularly remarkable about it. The students were forever bringing in their girlfriends during the day. So what could happen during the night that could not, just as easily, happen during the day?

Nancy turned to Ann. 'How did you feel about it?' 'I agreed with Richard. I loved it. We weren't doing anything wrong.' 'But that,' I said, 'is when the balloon went up. Somebody reported it to Father Tom. The change in him was dramatic. All that sense of freedom suddenly disappeared. He said we had compromised the reputation of Church Hostel, whatever that meant. He reported us to Sir James Ellison, the college principal and we were both rusticated for the rest of the term. It was a bitter moment when I had to explain this to my father.' Ann shook her head. 'My mother decided I should never see Richard again.' 'But punishment did a great deal more than that,' I said. 'We were allowed back the following term. But we both failed our exams as a result.' 'That is why,' Ann said, 'I ended up teaching Maths in Yorkshire at a girls' private school.'

'It left me,' I said, 'with a dilemma. If we had compromised the reputation of Church Hostel whatever that meant, so, in no uncertain terms was it even more compromised by Father Tom. There always had some extraneous man staying overnight. Usually he joined us breakfast. Father Tom's conquests came in all sorts and sizes. Some of them were members of the college. It left me wondering why he had the temerity to punish us.' Nancy chuckled. 'Perhaps his real reason was a fit of jealousy. As I said, you're an attractive young feller. He probably wanted you for himself.' 'You can understand,' Ann said, 'why I continue to detest Father Tom.'

'There was also a further point to it,' I continued. 'Homosexual acts were against the law. I could have reported his affairs to the police.' Nancy nodded. 'Why didn't you?' 'The evidence was circumstantial,' I replied. 'It would require proof.' I thought a moment. 'Apart from that I think it's wrong. A man should not be prosecuted for his sexual predilections. Added to that I owed him the vision of my vocation. I could not betray that.' 'That's all very well,' Nancy replied, 'but he betrayed you.' She turned to Ann. 'Why didn't you report him?' 'Richard could offer some sort of evidence. I couldn't.'

But there was a glint in Ann's eye. 'Richard took his revenge,' she said. 'Tell Nancy what you said.' It continued to amuse me. 'Father Tom was really vindictive when I returned to Bangor the following term. He arranged for my student grant to be cut off. I was longer allowed to stay in Church Hostel, though I was expected to pay the fees. Father Tom said it was to balance the books. The whole episode was depressing. I was obliged to move into digs, which put me at the mercy of a ferocious landlady called Myrtle. Even her fried eggs were undercooked. But it gave me an idea. When push came to shove Father Tom and Myrtle were in the same business. So I called him a "a glorified landlady".' Ann laughed. 'It was double-edged compliment,' she said, 'casting aspersions on his sexuality.' She smiled. 'Father Tom did not survive long after that. I have no idea whether it had anything to do with us. But he too was rusticated, banished to a small parish near Criccieth.'

'It sounds a complete mess,' Nancy said. 'But I think there's something to be made of it. You know me. I take a simple view of life.' She turned to me. 'I remember what you told me about Father Tom's preaching. It seems obvious. The students were young and susceptible. So he harnessed their romantic desires to his vision of divine love. That "Love Divine"[133] hymn does the same thing. That is why they 'flocked to hear him.' She looked pleased. 'You have to think about the making of a love affair. At first, it's very romantic. A young man believes he has found a goddess. Only later does he discover she's a girl. So Father Tom exploited their idealism.' 'There was,' I said, 'a little more to it than that. At that age love affairs come and go. He also exploited their sense of guilt.'

Nancy turned to me. 'You say Father Tom stimulated your vocation. But things have now moved on. Your vision of the goddess has long disappeared. You know what Ann is really like.' She smiled. 'I've heard your occasional sermon. You preach, I think, very well. But what, in general, do you talk about now?' I thought of Jesus' encounter with the Samaritan woman at the well. 'The words and works of Jesus of Nazareth,' I replied, 'his relationship to us and to the people of his day.'

Ann and I spent some time talking about it later. 'I had a feeling Nancy was going to surprise us,' I said. 'She's like the witches in Macbeth, forever given to stirring the pot.

133 *A&M Revised*, 205

But it was worse than I thought. I didn't want our problems at Bangor raked up all over again.' Ann was philosophical. 'Our lives since haven't come out too badly,' she said. 'At least we've got our degrees.' It amused me. 'So far as I'm concerned, a degree doesn't much matter. The church treats graduation as an IQ test. You've passed your exams, so must be intelligent.' It annoyed Ann. 'From what I've seen of it nothing the Church does shows the slightest intelligence,' she said. 'You're given all that training, all those studies in this and that, to say nothing of the bishop with his pomp and ceremony. It's made to sound so important. But when you're confronted with a dying girl in the hospital, all you have at your disposal is the Lord's Prayer.'

She thought a moment. 'But there's also another problem,' she continued. 'I'm inclined to trust Nancy. But what happens if she decides to tell people about our problems in Bangor. It was all very innocent. But the story can be easily misconstrued.' 'I don't really care what they think,' I replied. 'What matters is what I'm doing now.' 'I've also been thinking about that,' she said. 'A lot of what you do doesn't seem particularly relevant, such as dealing with the clearance of gravestones or resolving the problems when lightbulbs are stolen from Courtaulds. Nor, I think, should you be bothering with the antics of Celtic saints or the difference between the Church of England and the Church in Wales.' She thought for a moment. 'As you know, I don't believe in any of that.' Suddenly she relaxed and smiled. 'Yet I've see what you do. It's remarkably useful. In nature, things are forever getting into a mess. It takes the carrion crows to clean it up.' She turned to me. 'It's good that there are people like you around. The clergy are the carrion crows of society.'

I thought again of the mismatch between my training and my ministry. 'An awful lot of what I learned at the college was important,' I said. 'But it is not particularly useful. And sometimes it leads to pedantry. There's an old French adage. 'A man has to be excessively learned in order to preach so badly.'[134]

134 *Il fallait savoir si prodigieusement pour precher si mal.*

CHAPTER 40

Whereunto

Whereunto shall I liken this generation?' said Jesus. 'It is like unto children sitting in the markets, and calling unto their fellows, and saying, we have piped unto you, and ye have not danced; we have mourned unto you, and ye have not lamented.'

Some pretend they're at weddings, others at funerals. And so, it was. I remembered my encounter with Nancy. I loved her ebullient common sense. But this could not have been more sombre.

'You must take my word for it,' said John William Faulkner. 'He was there at every service. He heard everything you said, every word you preached. Yet you could not have known he was there. He was lurking in the porchway, too ashamed ever to come into the church.'

A man lurking in the shadows? It came as a complete surprise. It was typical of New Brighton. Never for a moment had I suspected that.

We were at the Church of St James to discuss the funeral of his nephew John Henry Faulkner, aged thirty-two, occupant of one of the narrow, terraced houses in the same row as the church. I had never met him. Apparently, he had died of a heart attack.

'He was quite young,' I said.

He nodded.

'In a sense, he had already passed away years before,' he said.

It sounded very strange. The rest of the story was no less bizarre. Some eight years earlier the deceased had fallen in love with Julia, quite the most beautiful young woman in the village.

'She really was splendid,' John William said. 'Blonde, elegant, not a hair out of place.' He shook his head. 'It was obvious for all to see. It was frightening. They could not keep their hands off each other. But Julia was his half-sister, born after his father had married again.'

So that was it, incest, the most powerful and ancient of taboos.

'What happened?'

'She died in childbirth,' John William said. 'They both died, Julia and her little girl. That was six years ago, six years and four months. He seemed to get over it at first, but it was not so simple as that. We hardly saw anything of him for months. He spoke to nobody, went out to work every day, came home and went to straight to bed. I tried to talk to him. He didn't want to know. He lost weight. He didn't seem to be eating properly. It was obvious. He was overcome with guilt. Then, whenever there was a service, he began to haunt the porchway of the church. You never saw him. Yet he was always there, too defeated, too overwhelmed ever to come in.'

'At least he went to work,' I said. 'What did he do?'

'He was a charge hand at the cement factory in Padeswood.'

I kept in touch with John William in the days that followed. The death was unexpected. There was a coroner's inquest. Ann had gone to see Val when John William came to see me at the flat.

'You will not believe this,' he said. 'He was my brother's son. Both his parents have passed away. I am the only relative. So, I went to sort out the contents of the house. It was a quite a mess.' His eyes lit up. 'Then it came as a shock. I could hardly believe it. I found money everywhere. There was money stuffed into his mattress, money hidden behind cupboards, crammed into drawers. You name it. Wherever I looked there was money. There were even bank notes behind a loose brick in the kitchen. I found literally thousands of pounds. And heaven knows where else it might be. What do you make of that?'

I had not the slightest idea. There was nothing else for it. We simply made arrangements for the funeral.

And so, we came to eleven in the morning, Friday, 24th July 1959, when once more John Henry, after six years of self-imposed exile, was brought through the familiar porchway into the chancel of the church. It was strange. As John William had said, he was there and he not there, the poor shattered remnant of a man. In some remarkable way, appropriately, the weather intervened, and it rained. It was sheer coincidence. I was reminded of the Wyncome funeral, but this was more persistent, the downfall torrential as I stood inside the doorway awaiting the arrival of the hearse.

What exactly had John Henry thought during those long, intervening years? And why did he hide the money? There was no means of knowing.

John William was at the organ, playing 'The Dead March' from *Saul*. The church was packed, not a seat to spare. People stood as I read out the sentences. Then, following the simple formal words of the liturgy, we went down to the cemetery for the interment. They came with umbrellas and raincoats pulled up over their heads. It rained, and it rained, and it rained.

When I was a student, I wrote poems that appeared in student magazines. I had since given up poetry, devoting my energies to developing the art of the pulpit. But this I was not going to pass up:

Beetles ate the woodwork
in the snail-trailed church.
Rain, like the dead
Marched over the roof.

Marching John Henry
away, away
into the grateful soil
by the drum of the dripping slate.

People remembered him,
in black abdication,
eating the words
of the Sunday-dry sermons.

Wind in the chimney
rustled the banknotes
stuffed behind bricks
in the narrow house.

Wind in his mind
delivered a child
again and again
in a childbirth death.

By the drum of the dripping slate
he went, washed by the rain
into the grateful soil
unexplained.

There was nothing more I could say about it than that.

CHAPTER 41

The fulfilling of the law

It was Ann who broached the subject. It had destroyed John Henry's life, but she asked, does that make incest a crime? I raised the point at the vicarage during our staff meeting the following Monday.

'The Church has always seen it as such,' the vicar replied, 'hence the "Table of Kindred and Affinity" at the end of *The Book of Common Prayer*. It tells us who we can and who are not allowed to marry.'

I laughed.

'But the relationships are so confusing. I was forever trying to work them out during my father's sermons when I was a child.'

'I agree, it is a bit of a labyrinth.'

I picked up a prayerbook and studied the list.

'They could surely have found simpler ways of expressing it. A man is forbidden to marry his wife's daughter's daughter. Presumably that means his granddaughter, unless his wife has been married before.'

He nodded and smiled.

'You can see the point. There's no simpler way of expressing it if you include the exceptions.'

'It's quite daft nevertheless,' I said. 'Think of the difference in their ages. What about a woman who wants to marry her son's daughter's husband?'

'In that case you will notice the difference. His granddaughter is a blood relative. Her granddaughter's husband is not. That's why the list is designated "Kindred and Affinity". But the law has changed. No longer do we take any account of "Affinity". It may not be a sensible thing to do.' He chuckled. 'But a man is not a blood relative to his wife's grandmother. So, if he's a widower, there's no legal reason to prohibit the wedding. The rule is simple. There should be no consanguinity between the partners to a marriage. You might find it difficult to believe that it was never before explicitly forbidden before, but a man is no longer permitted to enter into a marriage with his father.'[135]

That I found bizarre. But it did not answer the question. On what premise was incest illegal?

Ann was intrigued. We pursued the matter further on my return to the flat.

'There is no vindication of it in *The Book of Common Prayer*,' I said, 'merely a blanket assumption that incest is a crime.'

'Where does the idea come from?' she asked.

We looked it up. The 'Table of Kindred and Affinity' was published in 1563, abstracted by Matthew Parker, the then Archbishop of Canterbury, derived from the rules laid down

135 *Consolidation of Enactments (Procedure) Act 1949*

in Leviticus. So, we turned to the biblical text . . . the edicts of which positively delighted her:

> *Thou shalt not uncover the nakedness of thy father's brother, thou shalt not approach to his wife: for she is thine aunt.*[136]

'Really?' she said. 'So, he starts by stripping his uncle pink, which is bad enough. Then he lays lustful hands on his uncle's wife, which is particularly terrible "for she is thine aunt"?'

I shook my head.

'It's bowdlerised. The former is incestuous. The latter is not. It does not resolve anything.'

She pursued it further.

'What does it say about incest elsewhere in the Old Testament?'

I was obliged to admit it.

'There is one prime example. The two daughters of Lot took it in turn on consecutive nights to get their father drunk to have their wicked way with him.'[137]

Ann wondered if it were possible.

'Was there no such thing as brewer's droop?'

'I don't think that's what the story is about,' I said. 'We're told they each bore a son. One was called Moab. The other was called Ammon. It's sensational. But perhaps it was

136 Leviticus 18,14

137 Genesis 19, 30–38

thought up to make bastards of their enemies, the Moabites and the Ammonites.'

It brought us back to the original question. Is incest a crime? We could discover no rational answer to that.

CHAPTER 42

The Beetle

It probably made no financial sense, but having failed with the debacle of the MG, I finally decided I should buy a car. The vicar was enthusiastic.

'You can arrange a hire purchase,' he said. 'The parish will give you a rise of stipend. It's time we did.'

He had recently exchanged his Ford Zephyr for a Volkswagen Beetle, on the face of it a comedown compared to the more salubrious vehicles he had owned before. I remembered in particular his Standard Vanguard, the most intimidating of his vehicles. But never was there a man more passionate about Beetles.

'That is what you must buy,' he said, 'the brainchild of Ferdinand Porsche. You will never find a better made car, brilliantly engineered with a trouble-free air-cooled engine. Your aunt's Ford Popular is done and dusted after forty thousand miles. A Beetle needs a hundred thousand before it's run in.'

I had my doubts about it, though. Apart from anything else a Beetle seemed back to front, not at all my idea of a car. Pete Williamson had told me about them. Designed at the behest of Adolf Hitler, the Volkswagen manufacturing facility at Wolfsburg had been offered to a number of British manufacturers after the war, all of whom had turned it down. More importantly, while the car was made with Germanic precision and engineering, there was an intrinsic defect to the design. The rear-mounted engine affected the weight distribution, rendering it an absolute demon on ice. Anchored by the tail, driving a Beetle under unstable conditions could be positively dangerous. Considerably more expensive than cars of a similar size, they were nevertheless sold in their millions appreciated for their sturdiness and longevity.

'I've seen such a car advertised in the Chronicle,' the vicar said, 'at the Anchor Garage in Chester.' He scanned the newspaper before reading, 'An unmissable bargain, in mint condition.'

He became quite excited.

'It's Saturday today. The showroom will be open. I will be happy to accompany you if you would care to take a look.'

There seemed no reason to refuse.

'I'll leave it to you,' Ann said. 'I know nothing whatsoever about cars.'

So, the vicar drove me into Chester, which was an odd experience in itself. The engine, for all the world, sounded like a mobile sewing machine. But it certainly got a move on. The salesman's eyes lit up as we appeared. We must have seemed like a Punch cartoon, a thin slimy man and two simpletons in dog collars.

'My name is James,' he said, rubbing his hands. 'Would you like to go for a little spin?'

'I'll drive,' the vicar said.

'Are you sure?' he asked. 'I could demonstrate some of the vehicle's finer points.' 'No. Give me the keys.'

But there is another way of understanding a Beetle's instability. The weight in its tail could be used as a fulcrum, so that momentarily we were driving in one direction only to be, at the blink of an eye, speeding off in quite another. Our trial drive was a *tour de force*. It was fast. It was frightening. It was German engineering at its best as the vicar slipped in and out of the gears . . . which would have been difficult in the Snipe and impossible in the Ford Popular. We surged forwards, dodged oncoming traffic, swerved to the left, doubled back, spun through a couple of roundabouts, then in an instant we were back in the forecourt of the Anchor Garage where it belonged. The salesman was reduced to a pale shadow of his former self.

We examined the car. It had been meticulously resprayed. I pulled out the spare wheel from the compartment under the front bonnet. There was a gaping hole underneath. The vicar delivered the salesman a penny lecture before we walked off.

The Beetle I bought was from Pete Williamson, a delicate pale green, for which I paid considerably over the odds.

But then something else happened, quite unexpected. I was wandering down the High Street one evening when a newsagent's placard caught my eye: 'MOLD DOCTOR MARRIES.' It hardly seemed possible. I picked up a copy of *The Liverpool Daily Post*, which gave me the details. They were thoroughly ill assorted, yet, for reasons unknown, Roger had married his housekeeper, the totally unsuitable Mrs Joan Wright.

Why had they not mentioned it? I had taken them to Vale Crucis only a few weeks before. Was it my fault? I had neglected Roger recently. Most of our evenings were spent with Ronnie and Val. They too had heard the news.

'She will inherit his estate,' Ronnie said. 'He has two sons by his first marriage. They will not like it one bit. There's a great deal of money involved.'

It was none of my business, nevertheless.

CHAPTER 43

The lot has fallen unto me in a fair ground . . .[138]

Never was there such a disaster as the Grand Summer Ball arranged by the Young Wives for Saturday 8th August. Their plans had begun innocuously enough. They asked me to find them a band. I approached the Dave Winchester Quintet from Wrexham. I knew the band-master because, at one time, I was responsible for booking them for the Saturday night dances at the university.

The day arrived. The musicians came. They set themselves up on the stage in that dreary ecclesiastical church hall. They played. But it was high summer, quite the wrong time of year, so nobody turned up apart from the Young Widges and their reluctant husbands.

Ann introduced me to Wendy, their treasurer, blonde, thin, rather grand, married to James Holland, the Flintshire County Architect.

138 Psalm 16, 6. It probably means you've won at bingo.

'We owe the band thirty-five pounds,' she said. 'We've yet to set up a bank account, but don't you worry. We'll see that you're repaid.'

It came as a shock. It had never occurred to me that I was expected to foot the bill. Nor did it seem to worry her. I was dismissed as she turned her attention to Val.

'I know what we can do. We'll arrange a fashion parade. That should draw in the crowds.'

I didn't even want to think about it. I could not afford such a frivolity.

There was amusement in Val's eyes as she turned to me and said, 'He won't notice it. We'll take the money out of Ronnie's petty cash.'

But, certainly, we were short of money.

'We've decided to forgo our annual summer holiday,' I told the vicar said when we met the following Monday morning.

It was a fact of life. I had paid for our honeymoon. Ann had spent her residual cash on paint and wallpaper. So, the vicar went off with his family while I got to know the locum, a talkative old priest from Chester abounding in stories about the famous people he'd met.

'I was once introduced to Tubby Clayton,' he said, flapping a hand excitedly. 'You know who I mean, one of the founding members of Toc H. He was inspirational as an army chaplain during the war. He used a carpenter's bench as an altar and attracted a great many young soldiers that wanted to be ordained.' Suddenly, there was a twinkle in his eye. 'After the armistice he requisitioned the old jail at Nantwich for use as a theological college. But nobody turned up for breakfast the following morning. They were all locked in their cells.'

But there was no stopping the Young Wives. They were like a runaway train.

'You don't have to worry about the money,' Val said. 'We're negotiating with Mrs Ellie Jones who has the lingerie shop on the High Street. Ronnie has known her for years.' A naughty, suggestive look came into her eyes. 'She makes most of her money from selling knickers and bras. But she also sells other things.'

Ann was as enthusiastic as the rest. I told her to take it easy, but I was wasting my breath. The show was to take place on the second Saturday in September.

'Not only do we receive what money we take at the door, but we get a percentage of everything she sells,' said Wendy Holland excitedly. She put a persuasive hand on my arm. 'Do you think we could arrange a bar license so that our customers can have a glass of wine?'

I talked to Mr Bithell about it. He was able to arrange it. I remained sceptical, nevertheless.

I went down to the Church Hall early in the afternoon on the day of the show. It was quite remarkable. There was a prodigious air of excitement about the place. The Young Wives had made hardly any effort when they were arranging the Summer Ball, but this time they had excelled themselves. Even the church hall was transformed. There was more to Victoriana than I thought. Ronnie's men had put in extra lighting, with spotlights to pick out the various little architectural features that had remained unnoticed before.

Nor were these efforts unreciprocated. The parade was to start at seven. By five in the afternoon a queue was already forming outside. That, though, was but the half of it. The whole town was inundated. There were matronly wives everywhere . . . smart young things in flashy dresses, animated schoolgirls in pigtails and hats. Never had I seen so many eager women in one place.

I went down to the church hall again at about six. I let myself in through the old vestry door at the back . . . from which I was immediately ejected, allowing me no more than a glimpse of a model in scanty underwear. Instead I was let in at the main entrance.

Neville Bithell was appointed master of ceremonies which, apparently, during rehearsal he had performed with aplomb. So, the parade came on, with strings of models pussyfooting the catwalk through the centre of the hall, though not all of them were the bright young things I had anticipated. Clothes and underwear of all shapes and sizes were on display. I saw Linda give the vicar an amused nudge as Mrs Henrietta Derby was paraded before them, a generously proportioned member of the Mothers' Union.

Mr Bithell announced the names of the models as they appeared. A pretty girl from New Brighton called Heather was dressed in a sailor suit. She was designated 'Saucy Sue'. . . it was quite near the mark. She was not entirely unsaucy in real life.

During the interval people queued for glasses of wine. At the end it was up to me to thank everybody, the models and, in particular, the Young Wives, for all that had been achieved. There were celebrations all round. There was an avalanche of money. Ronnie's petty cash was reimbursed. The event was reported the following day in *The Liverpool Daily Post*, featuring a model in the skimpiest of bikinis.

CHAPTER 44

And nightly pitch my roving tent . . .

I met Jim Partridge one day on the High Street, erstwhile Vicar Choral at St Asaph Cathedral. I knew him from our student days. We discussed this and that before he broke the news.

'I've left the Church in Wales,' he said. 'It's no more than a backwater. I have decided to join the Roman Catholic Church.'

There was nothing I felt I could say. Some people need the certainty that the papacy inspires. I wished him luck. I didn't see him again for several months. Then, one day we met him while Ann and I were out shopping in Chester. It was astonishing. In a matter of months, he had both joined and left the Roman Catholic Church.

'All that business about the pope,' he said, 'is a load of rubbish. No man can know the mind of God.'

With that I was inclined to agree.

'What are you going to do?'

'I will join the Greek Orthodox.'

I wished him luck as before.

A few days later I received a letter from Williams, Jones and Davies, solicitors of Wrexham Street, giving me a month's notice to the effect that Dr and Mrs Roger Parker required us to vacate our flat. No reason was given. Ann was annoyed. I thought of having it out with Roger. There was no reply when I went round to the back door. Nor did I receive a reply at the front. I was sure they were in.

I went to see the vicar about it. He didn't seem in the least surprised.

'I've always liked Roger Parker,' he said, 'A thoroughly nice man who, in his day, was a quite excellent doctor. But it was notorious. His first wife used to order him about. Now it seems it is happening again.' He seemed undisturbed. 'No doubt people will have told you about it. The end section of this vicarage was separated off years ago to make accommodation for the curate. We'll have to move Linda's mother out so that you can move in. We'll find room for her somewhere else in the house.'

At least the problem was resolved. It was a relief, though I had mixed feelings about it. I had never liked the building from the start, but it seemed we had no choice. The vicar didn't seem in the least concerned by the fact that we should already have been living there rent free. But there was another, rather embarrassing, aspect to it all. We had virtually no furniture of our own apart from the two Ercol armchairs that replaced the Danish chair. So, we would have to make use of what was there, the property of Mrs Victoria Perkins, the vicar's mother-in-law.

We made the move the following week. That we had the Beetle made all the difference. Ann held the fort while I shunted to and fro with our possessions. Fortunately, I was able to arrange a hire purchase, so we bought a carrycot and a new double bed for ourselves.

There was one advantage to our living in the vicarage. From the front lawn we had a panoramic view of the town. On second thoughts, I did not dislike the building as much as I thought. I looked it up in Archdeacon Thomas' history of the diocese. Not only had Anne Davies of Llanerch instated the notorious 'man with the egg' but, in the same period, had paid for the building of the present vicarage, replacing the mediaeval establishment entitled 'Croft y Vicer'.[139] It explained the box-like rooms, typical of the late eighteenth century. There had been further changes since. Buildings had been required for the vicar's horse and carriage before the invention of the car. It explained the derelict buildings of the old institute.

139 the vicar's pasture

CHAPTER 45

The preparations

In November, we were visited by Mrs Eliza Jenkins, a tall, expressionless lady in a dark grey dress who introduced herself as the district health visitor. I had no idea such a profession existed. But there was something reassuring about her. Ann was getting larger and more misshapen by the day.

Mrs Jenkins was full of questions. The welfare of the baby was paramount, though she also expressed an interest in us as parents. Did Ann attend the antenatal classes? Did she have problems with her blood pressure? Of more immediate importance, was the curate's section of the vicarage suitable for the accommodation of a child? Each of our amenities was ticked off in turn, the kitchen, the laundry facilities, the heating system . . . everything.

'When exactly is the baby due?' she asked.

He or she was expected in the first week or second week of January. At the end of the inquisition our home was declared suitable, which hardly came a surprise.

'What,' I asked, 'would happen if the place wasn't up to scratch?'

'The baby would be taken into care,' said Mrs Jenkins.

But that was nothing like so alarming as the second set of enquiries we received later that day. There seemed to be nothing to it at first. The front doorbell rang. Parked outside was an orange Hillman Minx. A large stumpy man in a dark brown suit introduced himself as Charles Grayling of Herbert Goldstein and Sons, a firm of Chester solicitors. He was quite aggressive. He practically invited himself in.

'You are the Reverend Richard Millree Hughes?'

Ann appeared as he opened his briefcase.

'I understand that you and your good wife, Mrs Ann Patricia Hughes, until recently rented a flat, the property of Dr Roger Edward Parker of "Mount View", Pwllglas, Mold. Is that true?'

'Yes.'

'Furthermore, that you were required to vacate the premises after the said Dr Edwards was coerced into marrying his housekeeper, formerly Mrs Joan Alice Wright of 10, Mill Street, Mold? Is that correct?'

I looked at Ann.

'We weren't told why we were evicted.' He turned to me. 'But the reason was perfectly evident. Not in a thousand years could you as a clergyman approve of such a thing. There was no church wedding. The poor man was dragged in his wheelchair into the registry office and harassed into signing.'

He handed me a sheet of headed notepaper.

'My company represents Dr Parker's sons, the aggrieved parties. The marriage must be declared null and void. It is a travesty of the law. No man should be forced into matrimony against his will. Nor should our clients forfeit the proceeds of his estate.'

I was not sure what to make of it. Was Joan Wright, as I still thought of her, so unscrupulous?

'There were times when she neglected Roger,' I said. 'But I don't think she could coerce him into marrying her.'

He glared at me.

'Of course, she did. He's a defenceless cripple.'

'What,' I asked, 'do you want from us?'

'You, sir,' he said, 'are a man of the cloth. You are expected to stand up for what is right, to see that justice is done when this matter is brought before the court.'

I did not like the sound of that. The vicar, I remembered, had declined to take issue with Courtaulds.

'And what happens if I refuse?'

He gave me a firm look.

'You will be obliged to give evidence. We will issue you with a subpoena and you will be treated as a hostile witness.'

He was remarkably insistent. He wanted me to sign some papers. I refused.

We discussed the problem endlessly in the days that followed. Then, after the service the following Sunday, I was approached by Clive, a pleasant young man about my age who worked for his father, the ubiquitous Horace James, a prominent solicitor in the town.

'We want you to drop in at our office tomorrow morning at about eleven.'

He said no more than that. I had always liked Horace James, a large, portly, noisy man, noted for his after-dinner speeches. One of his oft repeated aphorisms I remembered particularly: 'I was guano-bombed by a seagull. I gave praise to God that cows don't fly.' But I was met with a quite different reception when I went in to see him the following day.

'Do not on any account have anything to do with those unscrupulous solicitors from Chester. Roger Edwards has decided to leave his money and his property to his new wife. Those sons of his don't have a leg to stand on. They may not like it, but it is his decision. Nor should they think his will can be overturned. It's watertight, witnessed by two of our local GPs.'

I was surprised at the vehemence of it.

'They want me to give evidence in court.'

He sat upright in his chair.

'I hope you will do nothing of the sort. Tell them they can go and whistle.'

'He became quite worked up,' I said.

Ann was unperturbed.

'No matter what happens, you can't be compelled into saying things. You must do what you believe to be right.'

But that was the problem. I could not sit in judgement. I remembered my reaction to the Assize Service. I knew nothing of Roger's sons. Nor did I feel any particular sympathy for the erstwhile Mrs Joan Wright. Perhaps Roger's marriage to her was a mistake, but if Clive and his father were right, he was not forced into it. It was not really any of my business. So, when the man Grayling came to see me again, I told him firmly to go away.

CHAPTER 46

The big world outside

The vicar told me about it. The story was going the rounds. Apparently, a couple of rather drunken B.B.C. Wales television reporters were wandering around the streets of Paris late at night. They were in the Rue Georges Bizet near the Greek Orthodox Cathedral of St Stephen, when they saw this apparition before them in the street, Makarios-like, in a long black cassock, flowing cape and luxuriant black locks. They found it quite funny. One of them said, 'Syt wyt ti, hen foi?'[140] . . . to which he was astonished to receive a reply in Welsh. It was Jim Partridge.

There was at that time a curious phenomenon. The streets were deserted every Tuesday evening between seven thirty and eight, not a soul in sight. There were plenty of people around at other times. But why? It took me some time to find out. Apart from Saturday afternoons when we went into the vicarage for tea, Ann and I had no access to a television. Ronnie laughed when I mentioned it. And so, it became clear. Everybody at that time on a Tuesday evening was watching *Hancock's Half Hour*. It seemed incredible that the

140 How are you old boy?

whole country should be fixated on a television programme, but it was. We went to Ronnie's to see an episode soon after, unravelling his antics as a blood donor . . . which made us, like the whole nation, in thrall of the incredible Mr Tony Hancock of East Cheam.

As before, on Friday evenings my time was taken up with the youth club. Afterwards, I was walking up the darkened High Street when a man appeared out of the shadows.

'Dr Roger Parker's wife is a golddigger.'

I was too surprised at that moment to be scared. I hardy saw him. I told him angrily to push off. It was the beginning of a pattern. From then on at the most unexpected moments, mostly late at night, I was further accosted by men with lurid tales of scandal about Roger's ex-housekeeper. It was worrying, it was disconcerting, it was muck-raking. Perhaps they thought as a clergyman I should be shocked.

'Try again to see Roger,' Ann said. 'It can't do any harm.'

So, I did. The Sprite was in the garage. The curtains to the living room twitched when I rang the front doorbell. Again, I got no reply.

I spoke about it to the vicar.

'I cannot believe I'm being pursued by private detectives.'

The word had evidently got round.

'I want you to take some time off,' he said. 'Go and stay with your parents. Remain there until things have settled down.'

It did not seem to resolve anything. 'But they're just as likely to find me at Llanrhaeadr ym Mochnant.'

He raised a hand.

'Just go.'

So, we found ourselves on an enforced holiday in my father's vicarage. The house looked rather different now it was furnished. But my mother was right . . . it really was a labyrinth. On the first floor the only way to the lavatory was though the central bedroom, which was probably used in the sixteenth century by William Morgan and his wife Catherine. Nobody slept there as a result.

Neither at the vicarage nor in the village at large was there any way of avoiding memorials to Bishop William Morgan. The council house estate was called Maes Morgan.[141] My younger brother Michael called it 'Rats Morgan'. He and his friends were at an unruly stage in their development, into eating sour apples and throwing stones. Then there was the William Morgan Memorial Village Hall. These associations with the great man excited a great deal of interest from outside the village.

'It's ridiculous,' my mother said. 'Sometimes, without so much as by your leave, we get busloads of people at the front door wanting to see the inside of William Morgan's house. It's what comes of living in a national monument.'

But the vicar was right. I was not again pestered by private detectives. So, having not had one earlier in the year, we treated the episode as a holiday. It was a period of respite. We went up the valley on a long meandering road to visit the Pistyll

141 Morgan's field

Rhaeadr,[142] the highest waterfall in England and Wales. The scenery is dramatic, with tall pines and lean bare hillsides drawing ever closer to the point where the water descends into a deep cleft at the end of the ravine. The cascade does not descend directly. Its fall is interrupted by a small reservoir two thirds of the way down so that the water surges before falling theatrically into the pool below.[143] We went down the rocky path to experience the force of it.

'You should understand,' I said. 'The Welsh word for 'pigs' is '*moch*' and '*nant*' means 'stream'. So, people think that the word 'Mochnant' is something to do with pigs. But there is a more ancient meaning to the word '*moch*'. It means 'swift'. Llanrhaeadr ym Mochnant is the village of the waterfall in the swift stream.'

About a week passed. We were enjoying ourselves, but as the legal problems had subsided, we were expected back in Mold.

'I'm pleased to tell you the opposition has given up,' Horace James said on our return.

142 I had seen a painting, attributed to Richard Wilson, among the exhibits at Chirk Castle which shows the waterfall descending into a pool populated with ships. Apparently, he had misunderstood a local farmer who suggested that his painting should include 'sheeps'.

143 The waterfall was visited by Dr Samuel Johnson while he was staying at the vicarage in 1774. To mark the occasion, the landowner, the fourth baronet, Sir Watkin Williams Wynne, caused the river to be dammed upstream. The water was released to coincide with the arrival of the great lexicographer.

CHAPTER 47

Christmas 1959

And so, we came again to the festive season, the flair, the carols, the tinsel, the birth of the child, anticipating too the birth of our child.

I had also become aware of the mood of the moment. New voices were raised, making their impact within the teachings of the Church. The time had come to demythologise, with shades of Dietrich Bonhoeffer,[144] to liberate Christianity of its legends. The Gospels of Matthew and Luke were written after the reign of the Emperor Nero.[145] In 65 AD, Nero was visited by Zoroastrian astrologists, which may be the origin to the coming of the Magi.[146] The mystery religion Mithraism was also in vogue, telling me how the god was born from a rock on 25th December. It explained the origins of the nativity narratives of Matthew and Luke.

It was time to bring Christianity into the real world. So, when I was invited to preach at St Mary's for the Midnight Mass, I did not hold back.

144 *The Cost of Discipleship*, 1937

145 Emperor of Rome, 54–68 AD

146 Matthew, 2

> *And Mary brought forth her firstborn Son, and wrapped Him in swaddling cloths, and laid Him in a manger, because there was no room for them in the inn.*[147]

'It's quite outrageous,' I said. 'A baby wrapped in swaddling cloths and laid in a manger surrounded by animal droppings. Any self-respecting health visitor would have the innkeeper arrested, the baby taken into care and Mary and Joseph sent on their way.'

147 Luke 2, 7

CHAPTER 48

The birth

Time seemed to go so fast. The Watchnight service had come and gone, and we were into the New Year. Ann was ultra large. Linda was forever in and out. All the arrangements had been made. I was not looking forward to it. When the time arrived, the moment of crisis, I was to take Ann to a maternity home near Chester. It was a bit of a blur when it finally happened. She uttered a loud moan. The vicar drove us in his Beetle while Ann and I sat in the back. No sooner had I handed her in at the maternity home that I was told to go away. Men were not allowed. Childbirth was a woman's business.

'It will take hours,' the vicar said. 'You had better come back to Mold with me.'

He could not have been more mistaken. We had arrived at the maternity home at about two. Our son was born just after seven thirty. By eight o'clock, in my own car, I was on my way back to the maternity home.

I thought about it as I drove. I was four years old when I first experienced the birth of a child. My sister Jean had been born two years earlier. I could not remember anything about it. But I was well aware of the birth of my sister Gill . . . the disruption, the fat midwife, the sheer panic as she dashed down to the kitchen for endless kettles of hot water. Gill's birth was a source of dismay. At first the baby was shut away in the upstairs spare room where she was born. From time to time we could hear her crying. When we were at last allowed see her, we were not in the least impressed. She was a nasty, noisy squealy little thing demanding every moment of my mother's attention.

I was twelve when my brother Michael born. The war was over. We had moved to Cilcain, and I was a pupil at the Alyn School in Mold. We were all entranced with the new baby. The parish was entranced. The whole world was entranced. For weeks my sisters and I walked on air, captivated by the perfection of his tiny hands, those miniscule fingernails. We were forever mapping out his future. What would he be? What could he be? These were my thoughts as I arrived to see our new baby. Ann was laughing when I went in to see her.

'Big Chief Sitting Bull,' she said.

And so he was, a tiny black-haired monster, some eight and a half pounds in weight, gifted with a powerful presence the moment he was born.

'He's beautiful,' I said.

'I wouldn't call him that,' Ann replied, 'but he's ours.'

We kissed. It was strange. He was no less remarkable than my brother Michael, but for the first time in my life, he was our responsibility.

At St Mary's on Sunday, 21st February, he was christened Mark Millree.[148] Our families and friends came together from all quarters to witness it.

148 My mother's maiden name. She was a lowlander Scot, though the name may have originated with the French 'Milroi'.

CHAPTER 49

The aftermath

We sat together quietly one evening. Mark was asleep in his cot. Ann was in a reflective mood. I poured her a glass of wine.

'Somebody said that a baby's eyes don't focus, that it takes them about a week to adjust,' she said.

'But babies still have inborn instincts. I remember what you said when we were on honeymoon, explaining why they can suckle from the start.'

She looked thoughtful.

'Can you imagine what it is like to be a baby?' said Ann. 'Your mind is a blank canvass. You don't even know you have parents.'

I laughed.

'My father went into a panic after I was born. I went blue and they thought I was going to die. My father christened me forthwith.'

'That's a parental reaction. You were told about it later. The baby would know nothing about it.'

She took a sip of her wine.

'That delivery unit at Mancot was disgusting. The place needs a good clean. I was lucky. Some of the women were in labour for hours. Mark was born quite quickly compared to some of the others. She hesitated. 'Have you ever thought about what it's like to be born?' she said, her eyes twinkling. 'It must be catastrophic . . . though, so far as I know, nobody ever remembers the experience.'

I had my own ideas about that.

'There is, I think a biblical folk memory about it, the first and most significant of all the legends. Adam and Eve, you remember, were placed by God in the Garden of Eden. I'm not sure about the serpent. It has, I think, sexual connotations. But as I understand it the garden represents the perfection of life in the womb. The baby is conceived. Nothing of it is required. That is paradise. The embryo grows. Then one day there's an explosion. The baby is thrown violently out . . . paradise lost.'

Ann was amused.

'You simplify the whole thing.'

'I don't think so. The Bible is quite specific about it.'

I turned to my copy of Genesis.

> *Therefore the Lord God sent him forth from the garden of Eden, to till the ground from whence he was taken. So he drove out the man; and he placed at the east of the garden of Eden Cherubims, and a flaming sword which turned every way, to keep the way of the tree of life.*[149]

149 Genesis 3, 22–24

'It expresses the dilemma perfectly,' I said. 'There is no way of going back into the womb.'

She studied my face.

'What I know about theology I've learned from you,' Ann said. 'The reason for it was Adam's original sin.'

I knew the answer to that.

'I don't think so. The feelings of guilt came later. You know how these legends evolved.'

She took another sip of her wine.

'What happened next?'

'It was, it is, difficult living in the world outside the womb: "Six days thou shalt labour and do all thy work."'[150]

Ann was amused. 'I don't believe in holy books, the Bible, the Quran or whatever, but they illustrate the evolution of ideas. But perhaps we do not need such books. A baby seems to go through the same process.'

I shook my head.

'There are far greater threats in real life. The Bible tells us that: "Wars and rumours of wars."[151] I remember when you talked about the fertile crescent at the end of the Ice Age. Not for a moment was it a recipe for peace, with the Egyptian pharaohs to the south, the Babylonians or the Assyrians to the north. The Old Testament is a history of war. Things have not changed since. Jesus was born in the

150 Exodus, 20

151 Matthew, 24, 6a

reign of King Herod the Great.[152] I continued 'Nor should we forget the arrogance of Adolf Hitler or Joseph Stalin.'

'The church also reflects it, the pomp and ceremony of popes and bishops,' she said impishly.

Now I was amused.

'While I was at theological college we were taught about the status of bishops. I've never heard so much rubbish in all my life. The rest of the clergy are mere acolytes. The bishops inherit the authority of the disciples with an unexaminable right to hold power over the church. It contradicts the teachings of the New Testament. Think of Jesus' encounter with Nicodemus. "The spirit bloweth where it listeth."[153] The history of the Bible is history of mavericks, like John the Baptist who went out into the wilderness, or Elijah in quest of the still small voice.'[154]

Nor should we forget Luther's resistance to authority at the Diet of Worms.[155]

She giggled.

'I know you don't like authoritarian bishops. I'm inclined to agree with you. They should be a thing of the past.'

She took a deep breath.

152 Herod died in 4 BC, making a nonsense of our dating system.

153 John 3, 8

154 All other Clergy and Officers of the Diocese derive whatever order of authority they may possess by devolution or delegation from the Bishop. Archbishop Green, *The Constitution of the Church in Wales*, 1937, p.100

155 Luther refused to recant at the Diet, a formal deliberative assembly called in 1521 by Charles V, the holy Roman Emperor.

'I remember what the vicar said on Whitsunday. The Holy Spirit is there to guide the Church. If so, it hasn't made a very good job of it. I don't know anything about the Celtic saints. They are your heroes. Nor perhaps does it matter.

'We've had a baby. We've been married for just under a year. I didn't always think so, but it has been the best year of my life. In some ways it has been quite weird. We were ejected from our flat. You were chased by private detectives. Some of the lessons read in the church were ridiculous. Miracles seem to happen at the drop of a hat. Did Jesus really cure a blind man by spreading his own spittle and clay on his eyes?[156] Who could possibly believe that?'

She paused a moment.

'But there's also something else. There are two things to say about the church. There are the beliefs and there is the social life. I think a lot of people attend the services because the members of the congregation are interesting and worth knowing. It's remarkable. Before we started the Young Widges most of them didn't come to church. They nearly all do so now.

'And what about you?' she continued. 'I don't know whether you'll ever get to heaven. I don't know whether there is a heaven, but what you do on earth is sufficient for me. You've been messed around from pillar to post. It doesn't seem to matter. You do your best to make sense of things, like the way you dealt with that incestuous affair at New Brighton.

156John 9, 6

And that poor girl dying of cancer in the cottage hospital . . . who else could have found a way to comfort her?' She gave me a sharp look. 'There, I've said enough. I don't think flattery does you any good.'

Postscript

For the moment my story is told.

The wedding of the century took place some fourteen months later. Her name was Philippa Davies-Cooke. She lived at Gwysaney Hall in the parish of Rhosesmor, some two miles from Mold. She was to marry William Warde-Norbury of Hooton Pagnell Hall near Doncaster, an officer of the Coldstream Guards. The ceremony was to take place at St Mary's on Friday, 15th April 1961, but it was a St Mary's transformed. The flower arrangers had occupied the church for three days. The end of each pew had its own unique posy of flowers. The pulpit was festooned with great banks of white lilies together with a million tiny forget-me-nots. Great hedges of blooms flanked the aisles, with dahlias, blazoning giant sunflowers and turgid red anemones.

'I have an important job for you,' the vicar said on the evening before. 'I will be conducting the ceremony. The bishops of St Asaph and Sheffield will be in attendance. You will supervise the signing of the register.'

I was intrigued. I tried to find out more. The bride belonged to one of the ancient families of Wales, descended in the twelfth century from Cymric Effel, one of the sons of Madog ap Maredudd, prince of Powys, which is perhaps why, at the turn of the eighteenth century, his descendant, Robert Davies of Llanerch, was an archivist and collector of rare Welsh manuscripts . . . to which must be added his significance as 'the man with the egg'.

But there were problems to do with the parish boundaries. It was not quite clear why. On the morning of the wedding a civil ceremony took place at the registry office in Holywell. It met the legal requirements.

The sun shone. The bishops arrived. The church was filled with the great and the good. To herald the arrival of the bride, James Dickens launched into the persistent arpeggios of Charles-Marie Widor's *Toccata*.

I listened to the music. But I saw nothing of the ceremony, ensconced by myself in a high-sided bower to the side of the font. At the end of the ceremony, the wedding party came to me. There is one rule to do with the signing of marriage registers. The Registrar General is most particular. The record has to be immaculate, not a word out of place. There was only one way of ensuring it. The entry is never to be filled in beforehand in case the couple fail to turn up. So, they stood there while I wrote it out. They then signed in turn, after which to reinforce it, the bridegroom kissed the bride. I asked the bride's father, Philip Ralph, how I was to enter his occupation.

'Gentleman,' he said.

After the ceremony, I collected the Beetle and followed the procession of cars to the reception at Gwysaney Hall. As at the church, no expense had been spared. It was positively mediaeval. Ann had been invited, but as she was in the advanced state of her second pregnancy, there was no way she could attend. Our son Jeremy was born three days later.

I had expected to see a marquee, but there were three, packed with tenantry from the two estates. Busloads had been brought down from Yorkshire. There were servants galore, handing out canapés and glasses of champagne. I did not fail to join in. There were police at the gates when I left. They waved me through. I should have been arrested. I drove home on a pink cloud.

Somebody said that, to pay for it, some of the archivist Robert Davies' manuscripts were sold to an American university. From what I know of them, they are in the National Library of Wales.

Printed in Great Britain
by Amazon

34697902R00158